ROGER $\mathcal{B}$
PRIVATE INVESTIGATOR

ACTION IS MY MIDDLE NAME

To: TAMI

I hope you enjoy this
book.
Like I enjoyed your
beauty
Enjoy!!

8-7-04   Paul Foster x.

ROGER $\mathcal{B}$
PRIVATE INVESTIGATOR

ACTION IS MY MIDDLE NAME

PAUL EUGENE HILL JR.

Published by Aventine Press, LLC
45 East Flower Street, Ste. 236
Chula Vista, CA 91910-7631, USA

www.aventinepress.com

ISBN: 1-59330-029-8

Printed in the United States of America

I dedicate this book to my mother, father, sister, grandmother, grandfather, and my family. But mostly I dedicate this book to the dreamers.

"Time is like rushing waves. It may slow you down from moving forward, but it will never stop you."

CHAPTER

1

ESCAPING THE RAPIDS

The setting seemed to be like that of a Tarzan movie. When the English people are on safari looking for elephant tusk. Everything starts off ok, then suddenly you're placed in a totally negative situation where it would seem to be the end. This is how my adventures started.

I guess I should introduce myself before I tell you my stories. My name is Roger "B". The "B" is another story. I'm a freelance detective living in Atlanta, Georgia. As a Native American, adventure is my life, as you'll soon see. Well, that's enough for now. So if you're ready, lets go on an adventure.

The story begins at base camp near the Sauk River, northeast of Seattle, Washington. Where a few people and myself were waiting anxiously to start exploring a few caves, do a little hiking, and my favorite since the age of six, white water rafting.

The wilderness was like home to me. It's the only place in the world that still moves slow. There's no concrete, just soft earth under your feet. The air is so fresh, that you can use it to flush the carbon out of your lungs from the city life. There is nothing here but the basic elements for survival. For the next couple of days I'm going to enjoy as much nature as possible.

"Hi, my name is Wendy. So what brings you here to these neck of the woods?"

"Hi, my name is Roger. Umm...the nature, and all the open area. So, you come here often?"

She laughed for a second and then said, "I hope that was a joke, but no. I don't get to travel that much, and a friend of mine couldn't make this trip. So, I decided that since he was offering a free vacation, I should take it."

"Is your friend sick?"

"No, he had other plans that came up all of a sudden."

"Ah...I'm happy that you could make it. Otherwise, I'd be here talking to your friend. And just between you and I, I think that your legs are much slender and sexier."

"Thanks, Oh! the lecture is starting."

We were being instructed by one of the guides to stay close and not to wander off too far during any of the hikes.

I was very busy skylarking to even be aware of the instructions that were being given at the time. One of the females that was in my group nudged me in my side so I would pay attention. There were only two guides, so we were paired off into two groups of four. Wendy was in my group.

"OK people, my name is Mr. Caroles. I'll be your guide. For those of you who have never been on a hike before, I have a few does and don'ts you shall be interested in. One, don't wander off. Two, if you are faced with any kind of danger from an animal out here and feel that your life is being threatened, just play dead and the animal will leave you alone. Three, don't wander off. These rules are for your own protection. Are there any questions?"

Given the opportunity I thought I'd lighten up the group by saying, "Yes, I have a question. If one of us goes to the bathroom, does that mean that we all have to go...you know...just to make sure that person doesn't wander off?" From his following looks, I don't think that he found the comment humorous. After his speech we were on our way for an enjoyable day. I looked at my watch and the time read 2 p.m.

A couple of hours had passed before we came to the jagged entrance of a cave. This was one of the sights for an Indian burial. The view from here was magnificent. I could see everything. To my right, past the tall pines was base camp, and to the left of that was the river. "My final glorious and lovely destination."

If you look down the path, you could barely see where it starts to turn into the rapids. Part of the river also flowed past the westward half of this mountain.,

We stayed in the cave for a few minutes, long enough to get a little history of the burials and who might be buried there. I'll have to find out later if this is one of the sights of my relatives. After awhile, I looked at my watch again and saw that the time was 4:59pm. By this time the guide was starting to sum up his story, so we could get back to camp for dinner.

Later that night after dinner everyone was telling their version of a campfire tale. Since I was not interested, I asked Wendy if she wanted to take a walk with me to enjoy the night air. We stood around taking deep breaths of the pine scents, it was so exhilarating. There was also a half moon out that seemed to be the spark for a good ghost story. As we walked away we made sure not to lose sight of camp.

"So Roger, are you enjoying the sights?"

Since I was facing in her direction, I replied immediately with a sharp, "Yeah!"

"I'm talking about the outdoors," she said, with a smile on her face.

"Oh! Of course; I was talking about the same thing," I said, while pulling my tasty leather boot out of my mouth.

She walked closer to me, grabbed my hand, sat me down beside her, and persisted in getting comfortable like a cat in a blanket. "Now that I'm warm, how about a ghost story?" she said, while I was focusing on her lips. Those were the next words I was hoping to hear, Not! But I told one anyway.

"On a cold and dark night like this one, fourteen years ago there lived a lumberjack named Bob the Bearen. No one ever talked to the Bearen. They feared him, because of the deformity of his face. He was a loner, who only came to town when he needed supplies.

"One day while the police were driving past the woods, they noticed that Bob's lights were on and his door was wide open. One of the policemen decided to take a look. After searching his house and the area, Bob was nowhere to be found. In the yard near a large tree was a puddle of blood. Pieces of material were shredded all over the place. Bob was never found and no one ever found out what happened.

"Two weeks after that night, on a winding stretch of road near Bob's old cabin, drove an old lady. She was on her way home. Ahead of her was a man walking on the side of the road. She hardly paid any attention to him as she drove by. A few miles down the road he appeared ahead of her again, walking aimlessly. Feeling a bit curious, she decided to stop. She pulled over and waited for him to catch up before she said, 'excuse me, do you need any help?' as he approached the passenger side. He just stood there. Her breathing started to thicken, as fear entered her mind for the first time. She lowered her head to get a better look at him. That's when she noticed the blood dripping from his neck. All of a sudden he shoves his head in the passenger window, and said, 'Yes! could you help me find my face?' It appeared that the flesh from his face had been ripped off. Without another second to spare, she drove off with the reminder of bloody hand prints on the door. Fearing that no one would believe her, she never reported what happened.

"Sometimes when people are hiking through these woods, they can hear Bob asking for help to find his face."

"THERE HE IS!" Wendy jumped straight up, and I started laughing. "Oh my goodness Roger, you really scared me. Thanks for the slight heart attack." After that we walked for a few more minutes, then decided to turn in.

The next morning I was told to go and retrieve some fresh water. On my way to the stream I imagined myself looking like a true sportsman during the rafting competition. Maneuvering the raft right, left, avoiding all the rocks in the way. Controlling every twist and turn conquering the devastation of the rapids. The guides called these rapids "The Wash Away Rapids." Because one wrong move, and that's exactly what would happen to any rafter.

This was the ultimate goal and challenge.

After breakfast, I chose to take a walk alone to help my food digest. Touring through the woods, I started to notice that every inch of the woods looked similar.

Afterwards the whole area became a maze, scene after scene. I had no idea where I was. It would have been quite simple to just look for the smoke from the fire, except for one small problem. Earlier when we finished breakfast, I was responsible for extinguishing the cinder and ashes. I continued to walk in one direction, in hopes of getting some kind of a clue for where to go next. I soon came to a cliff. "Now I am lost." It was a steep cliff, a cliff to the imagination reached higher than any skyscraper. Especially since the bottom was nowhere in sight. If that wasn't enough, out of nowhere came a mountain lion, and beyond him somewhere past the trees, was my freedom.

I remember the guide saying to play dead and the animal would go away, but by the look in this cat's eyes, he was there to stay. So I did the next best thing, I waited. Patience has never been my strong point, but that day I had a little extra boost that provided me with enough patience to wait out a war.

As time progressed, the mountain lion started getting another look in his eye. This one was the look of a villain in the Wild West, who was about to set his guns blazing, as he charged me. So I took one

step forward, which caused him to take a
few steps my way. "Not good," I thought.
Suddenly, I heard a sound coming from the
bushes behind this massive cat. "Yes, I'm
saved," crossed my mind, and a sense of
peace consumed my fast beating heart. You
would think that soon, all of this would
be considered a nightmare or a bad dream,
right! No, because instead of who I was
expecting, it turned out to be another
mountain lion. Two hungry mouths coming my
way. "Where is that medium rare steak when
you need it?" I always thought that if I
died, it would be fast and painless. "The
river below is probably not that deep, so
if I jump, I may not survive the fall,"
is what I was thinking long and hard on.
Well, it seemed long, because every second
brought me closer and closer to my death.

   I turned around, closed my eyes, and
said a prayer while I was taking a leap of
faith. In no time at all I was submerged
in an ice cold river. Cold enough to send
me into shock, because for a while I felt
that time had stopped, and there was
nothing happening. I envisioned myself to
be dead, and had not yet passed over to
the other side. I was not sure.

   Then I began to sense my movement. "I'm
alive!" I thought while floating down
the river. "Yes, I'm safe," ran through
my mind, until I realized that I could
drown in here. I tried to make my way to
the top of the water. After awhile I made
it. Which was just enough time to prepare

myself for what lie ahead. Not too far was a tree that had fallen across the river. That's when I realized why it took me so long to get to the top of the water earlier. My right shoulder was dislocated. Therefore, in order for me to reach the branch that was hanging down, I would have to shift my body around, and grab hold with my left hand. My, can't catch a ball hand. No time for error today. If I can't grab this branch I'm gone for sure. This wasn't my only problem. I also had to worry about keeping myself afloat. "OK, now or never." I tried to stay steady while bobbing up and down. "No! I missed it," but at that same instant I was caught by someone's hand.

"Is it too premature to think to myself that I was finally safe? Maybe, but by the looks of things I would have to say no." I was pulled to shore by a strange man who I had never seen before. He gave me a blanket to cover up with. He turned out to be a rescue ranger.

Later, at the hospital, I was told that the rescue team was called by some hikers who had reported me missing. The rescuer, whose name was Alex, told me that they had spotted me on the cliff shortly before I jumped. "If I had to guess I would say that you are one lucky person. Jumping from that cliff, and surviving is a prayer answered" said Alex. I was also told that Wendy was the one who had reported me missing. "I truly am one lucky person."

That afternoon, Wendy came by after conquering the rapids. She was happy that everything turned out alright. She said she was on her way back home, and just wanted to drop through to say bye. So before leaving we shared one last kiss to wish each other good luck in life.

CHAPTER 2

THE BIG SCOOP

She was your average smart and witty blonde-haired person, who had a nose for trouble. Then again, what reporter do you know that doesn't. Shelly Turner worked at the 'Atlanta Press Times', which was a small newspaper company. When she wasn't getting any big action, she'd take other stories on the side. I guess this was her way of living life to the fullest.

On Monday evening she received a telephone call that sounded like trouble from the first ring. It was a private informant who called about some kind of story in Texas. Did I fail to mention that she loved the value of a dollar, $10,000 for this story to be exact? When the stories had a high price, it usually meant trouble. Trouble with a dollar sign written all over it.

Soon after hanging-up the telephone, she called an airline agency and booked a flight for the following day. I thought to myself that I was due for a vacation, so I told her to make reservations for two.

Being the witty person that she is, she said, "Are you sure you're old enough to go flying off into trouble?"

To which I replied, "Being a grown man makes me legal, besides, it's you that's going to be needing a babysitter."

We arrived Tuesday afternoon, when no sooner did the trouble start. She received a call at the airport from the informant that there was to be an illegal alien movement and a shipment of guns being transported to Texas from Mexico in two hours.

We made our way towards a car rental to acquire some wheels. What do you know, today is a discount day for foreigners, "Rent a car today and pay for the problem that comes with it tomorrow."

On the way we ran into a little trouble. The kind that only a man of my skill could fix. That's right, you guessed it, a flat tire. No wonder the rental place was so cheap.

Shelly was so afraid that she would miss out on the excitement that she started walking down the road, and yelling for me to just pick her up when I finished with the tire. No sooner than she said this, the tire was replaced, and we were back in business.

We finally arrived at the location, but saw no signs of any kind of transport vehicles of any sort. Speaking of no sign, this had to be the most deserted place I've ever been in. I know that a dessert is supposed to be empty, but this was a sad sight. I didn't see any tumbleweeds or buzzards flying around or old people begging for water. It was just a bunch of nothing. Shelly was worried that we had arrived too late. She said, "Damn, I really need this money. How else am I going to be able to afford the new condominium I bought. I knew it was a bad idea to allow you to come along. You're the only person I know that could ruin a wet dream."

No sooner than she said this (and I won't forget that it's my turn to make a wise crack about her good luck), from out of nowhere came two large trucks with tarps over the back of them. "What do you think, is that them?" I said to her. We took cover behind the S.U.V. (to those who don't know what this is, it's a sports utility vehicle). We allowed them to get some distance between us before pursuing them. I didn't think it would be a good idea to drive close enough to read their bumper sticker that probably said, "Alien-transports are us."

As we approached an abandon town, the trucks were being unloaded. If I had to count, I would say it was about thirty people that got out of the back of the truck. We stopped behind an old hotel, and walked towards a warehouse where the transaction was taking place. I'm guessing that after the transaction, the aliens

would collect their fake I.D. and filter
into Texas.

Hold onto your hats, because here is
where it gets dangerous!

Spotted by one of the truckers, we
headed for cover, due to the too close
for comfort factor. One of the truckers
pulled out a bazooka and fired at us. They
blew up the crappy rental and part of the
hotel. This situation reminded me of the
time I was in the Marines. (During basic
training, I was told to go through an ob-
stacle course as part of my evolution to
become a "REAL MARINE." I refused to go,
so my drill sergeant grabbed his .45 and
started firing it into the air, needless
to say I set a new record for clearing
the course and crossing most of the base.
Anyway, I was scared.) We made our way
into the warehouse, where I encountered a
striking bit of trouble.

Bitten by a rattlesnake just seemed to
be my luck. In fear of the poison I pulled
down my pants and saw that I was bitten
just above the knee, on my inner thigh.
I looked at Shelly and said, "Shelly, I
know that we haven't been all that close,
but if you suck out the poison I won't
tell." Hesitant at first, she knelt down,
compressed the inner thigh, and started
sucking the wound.

(Don't forget we're still being chased
by the truckers.) They realized that we
were trapped in a room, so they locked
the door, and set the warehouse on fire.

There's nothing better than being bit by a snake, trapped in a warehouse, that's on fire, and if that's not enough, the building was starting to collapse. "What else could happen to ruin such a beautiful day?" I said.

Followed by Shelly who said, "Why did you say that Roger, you know something else is going to happen now? Well, I really can't blame you for what happened here. Besides, because of you, I haven't had this much of an adventure since I started reporting."

Shelly felt a draft coming into the room and noticed a grid that covered an underground shaft beneath the floor. I told her, "Now I know why I like you so much. You always know how to get out of the tough ones." We made our way through the shaft. Shelly went first and I was behind her.

Meanwhile, because of the earlier fireworks, set off by the two truckers, the police had decided to join the party. (I've never known any doughnut shop that had been robbed successfully like that of a bank, or a jewelry store. They are so on time.) The illegal aliens were rounded up to be taken back to Mexico. The two truckers became part of a high-speed chase, which drug the police all across the dessert. I assume that the truckers knew the territory, because as they were being pursued they caused one police officer to run into a ditch, and another one to somehow run into a big boulder that was sticking out of the ground. After awhile the pursuit ended in a bitter loss for the police. Yes, the bad guys got away. What a surprise.

We were still making our way out of the cramped situation when I started to feel a little dizzy. Finally, we were out in the middle of nowhere. Shelly realized I was looking somewhat faint, so she grabbed me by the waist and draped my arm around her shoulders. The sun started to go down and since we had missed the festivities, there was no one around to take us back to town. I started shaking because of the drop in temperature, so when we spotted an area full of large rocks we decided to stop there for the night. Before going to sleep I told her that I owed her big time, and I was happy that she was a woman and not a man, because I don't think I could share body heat with another man. Especially that snake bite incident.

While I was asleep, Shelly was arranging her thoughts for the story she would write. She was happy that she had brought a concealed camera to take the pictures of the two truckers and the activities that went on before we were shot at.

Morning arrived, and I was still dizzy from the snakebite. We got up, and walked to the highway and after about one hour of walking we caught a ride with an old man in a rusted truck with a logo on the side of it that read, "Orange you glad we picked them." He was more than happy to give us a ride into town. Shelly told him that I had been bitten by a snake and was seeking medical attention. He increased his speed, but for some reason it seemed like we traveled at a snail's pace. Once we got to the hospital and I was treated, life felt a whole lot better.

Anyway, Shelly got her story and the little dollars that makes it worth her while. After the ordeal in Texas I decided to take a little vacation in the hospital. You never know when you're going to need a doctor.

You know what, getting in trouble might become a career for me.

CHAPTER 3

REMEMBER THE PAST

"I've always enjoyed getting together with old friends. We'd sit around and talk about the old times and the things that were going on then. Little did I know, that my next get together with an old friend would be the kind of reminiscing anyone could do without."

Shawn Garrett was my best friend in high school. We always hung out together no matter what. I guess it was because he could make me, and anyone, laugh all the time. He was always doing something stupid. His jokes were unforgettable, especially if the joke was on you.

I remember one time in high school when Shawn told me that his locker was broken and he couldn't put his books in it. He was late for class and asked if he could use my locker for the rest of the day. I said yes in an unsuspecting way, not knowing that Shawn had something fishy up his sleeve. I gave him my combination and proceeded to my class.

It was the end of the day, and I noticed a few people standing around my locker, people whose locker was no where near mine. I paid them no mind as I walked up to the locker.

It was three o'clock and I was ready to go home. Oddly, one of the guys asked if I was having fish for dinner that night. Since I didn't understand his question, I proceeded to open my locker door. There it was, the answer to the riddle, a three pound fish was hanging over my books. The smell drove most of the guys away, and the others just stood there laughing at me. Because of the smell I had to move to another locker. It took three days to get that smell out, and my books had to be replaced. I figured the heat from the outside of the school, and the heat from my locker caused the smell to grow increasingly toxic. I thought to myself, "There's nothing like a good friend."

Shawn is now living in Aruba, and he asked me to come down and watch him compete for a chance to qualify for the Olympics in table tennis. I said yes, because I was happy to know that his life didn't turn out to be like that of a drug dealer or some type of a criminal. He even sounded very serious about the sport on the telephone. I was proud of him. From that point, I changed the way I thought of him.

I guess it's not fair to judge someone from the things that they have done in the past. If Shawn could change, then there's hope for anyone.

My flight to Aruba was rather comforting, thanks to Catherine the stewardess. She saw to it that my pillow was fluffed, and requested that the one in my room be fluffed by her as well. She said that she had a layover on the island, and wanted to spend whatever time she could with me. I told her that I was on my way to visit a friend, but that I would be happy to see her while she was there. She had the kind of glow that made you want to look around for a movie camera. She had an unbelievable smile, and the quality you could only find in a movie star, or a model. At the same time she was so polite, well mannered, and seemed to carry herself like it was nobody's business. "If I play my cards right, maybe my luck will change."

At the airport, I went to retrieve my baggage when fate struck. I was told that my luggage, somehow was not put on my flight, and could possibly be on its way to Kansas. "Out of all the places, why Kansas," I said. Before I find anymore trouble, I think it would be best if I went straight to my hotel, which is probably on fire right now as I speak. I exited what seemed to be the front entrance to the airport, but turned out to be a side exit, which lead to a row of cabs. On the other side of the cabstand was a limousine driver, who was holding up

a sign with my name on it. So I walked up
to the limousine driver and said to him,
"I hope you don't have a gun or a bomb or
some poison in your car waiting for me.
Today has not been good to me." I told
him that I wanted to go to the hotel first
before going to Shawn's house. It seemed
pretty strange that shawn could afford
a limousine to pick me up, and drive me
around without any practical jokes happening.

On the way to my hotel, we made small
talk about the island. He told me about
the ANTILLA, which was a freighter in WW
II. It was used to supply German subs.
Because of her elusiveness, to not be
caught, she was nicknamed the GHOST SHIP.
Later, she was surrounded by the local
authority and was ordered to give up. The
captain was unwilling to turn her over
so, he went down to the engine room, and
over-pressurized the boiler system so it
would blow. She now sits fifty to sixty
feet under water, off the southern coast
of Aruba.

I figured the reason for the story-
telling was, because this was the sight
that we would be diving at tomorrow.
Right now, I had my mind set on taking
Catherine to those white sand beaches, and
to the casinos. We finally arrived at the
Oranjestad Beach Resort. As I was checking
in, the limousine driver approached me
with a message from Shawn. It said that
he had some sort of business to take care

of, and would have to take a rain check on today's plans, but would meet me tomorrow for a deep sea adventure. "Adventure," now there's a word that seems to follow me wherever I go. So I sent the driver away, and went to my room to freshen up. This was my first night in Aruba, and I wasn't going to spend it alone. The first thing I needed to do was, go shopping, and since there was a small clothing shop on the first floor of the hotel I didn't have to go far.

After going shopping, and taking a shower, I called Catherine. We met at a casino two blocks from the hotel. I was really enjoying myself with her. I found out that she, and I had so many things in common. For example: she likes to swim for exercise, she likes sushi, and she likes to be shot at, chased and almost be blown-up. "Just kidding, those are some of my likes."

We hit it off rather well. Later that night we took a stroll along the beach. She said that I sparked an interest in her, and that she was woman enough to take a chance to see if that spark could start a fire. Considering the fact that she had nothing to drink earlier, I knew she wanted me.

Then she said, "I once had a dream about making love on the beach. Since we are here, you can make my dream come true." I took her in my arms and we started to kiss. First we started out with soft,

gentle kisses, while our hands caressed
the contour of each other's body, rubbing
one another like two blind people trying
to find our way around each curve, and
each soft texture. Her breathing began
to deepen. After a while we started to
kiss like wild animals trying to tear
each other apart. We paused long enough
to make our way into a surfboard shed.
There, we held nothing back. Tearing each
other's clothes off became competition.
She wanted me as much as I wanted her.

I couldn't help myself for the way I
looked her up and down. She had a skin
tone the color of bronze from head to toe,
and the kind of curves like that of a dan-
gerously winding road. Her breasts stood
up like two firm springtime melons, with
two light pink nipples that were waiting
to be substitutes for a cherry pop cycle.
She had the kind of lips that blossomed
from her face with the most perfect
shape. Her eyes were as dark a the street
pavement or coal, with a little slant, as
if to possess a hint of Asian. Her body
was like a work of art. I felt our bodies
join together to create enough friction
to heat the sun up. Sweat came from our
pores as if we were taking a shower. We
held each other so tight that we squeezed
the life out of each other several times.
There was no comparing this event to any
past affair. Our hearts were beating to
the same drum. I looked deep into her eyes
as she said, "I know this affair can't

last for long, but I'm willing to reserve a place for you in my life if ever we meet again." I told her that it's not everyday that I'm in a shed making out with a beautiful woman, and since neither one of us had games on their mind, this night means a lot to me.

As the heat, and smoke died down from our love making, we helped ourselves to a few minutes of bliss before leaving. I walked her to the street to catch a cab. On the way there we exchanged compliments on the fire works we had ignited. One kiss for the road and she was on her way back to her hotel. "Don't worry, we will be seeing each other again, but right now, I have a meeting with my mattress."

The next day I got a call from Shelly, who was back in Atlanta. She had called to see if I was OK, but what she was really asking me was, is there a story there, and is there any money to be made. I told her from the look of things, this island is the most peaceful place on earth right now, and there's nothing going on. Then she responded by saying, "First of all B, wherever you are, peace is on the opposite end. The two of you just don't mix. That's OK, I'm quite sure that when you return, you will have a story to tell me." I laughed snobbishly as if to say, "Whatever." We talked for a few more minutes then I told her I had to go. So she said, "Bye, loser," which to me meant, I miss you, and be careful.

Seven o'clock in the morning rolled around, and I had just finished taking a shower when the telephone rang again. It was the front desk calling about the limousine driver, he was outside waiting for me. I hurried up, and got myself together and rushed out the door. My mother would always say, "If you leave the house in a hurry, make sure that you wear clean underwear because you never know when something is going to happen to you. Besides, that's less money we would have to spend on your funeral." Sometimes, I think she was serious.

I arrived at Shawn's house, and was immediately impressed at the fact that he had come so far from being this silly little jokester, to owning a three story house with a classic contemporary style. In the back was an oval shaped pool with a poolside bar. The inside of the house was even more impressive. The downstairs floor was covered with oak wood, the living room was decorated with British Colonial furnishings, joined with antiques. Every fireplace in the house was shadowed with 19th century Italian works of art. The dining room table, which a drop-top Louis the XIV allows four to twelve guests to dine.

We sat out back at the poolside bar and talked about the times that had passed between us after high school. Shawn talked about his love for table tennis, and how he came to love it so much. He

said, "While I was in college, I met a
woman that changed me forever. She didn't
mind the childish side of me. Actually,
she would sometimes encourage it. She said
it was healthy to laugh. After a while, I
would do things intentionally to get her
to laugh, but I also wanted her to see
my mature side. Therefore, I would make
serious faces as if to say, I'm only 99.9
percent childish. College became more of
a place to be, because she was there, and
not because I needed an education.

Two years later she died of cancer. I
became enraged with life, and started
drinking a lot, as well as hanging out
around the wrong people. I also started
borrowing too much money, money that I
couldn't pay back. Anyway, table tennis
became my way of relaxing, and soon became
a passion." All at once he became silent,
not a word came from his mouth. Feeling
his sadness, I picked up the conversation.

As if whatever I had to say would
cheer him up. So I started by saying,"I
never had the chance to leave Atlanta,
that's why I'm still there. I also went
to college, but found no love as the one
that you have experienced. I got a degree
in Criminal Law, but instead of becoming
a lawyer, I decided to be a private investigator. Which gives me the freedom
to live my life on the edge, or just experience whatever life has to offer me.
Being a freelance detective doesn't help

me to live lavish or provide me with lots
of money, but I manage to get by. So
far, I can't say I'm bored, believe me,
there's a lot going on in my life to say
the least."

Feeling like two women telling stories,
I quickly changed the tone. After a few
more hours of talking, we decided to head
down to 'ANTILLA.' I would finally get
some great scuba diving done, and if the
ocean scene is anything as he described
it, I'm in for a treat (hint).

On the way down to the marina, Shawn
was short of conversation. He acted as if
there was something on his mind. I asked
what was wrong, but he would just say that
it was about business. Again, I asked,
what kind of business, but like before he
was short of words. He tried not to let
his worries show, but being the true detective that I was, I saw right through
him. He also had sweat on his forehead.

We finally arrived at the marina. Shawn
went into a small office, on the way he
asked me to go help get the gear ready,
and said that he would be there shortly.
I walked down the boardwalk until I was
facing a massive yacht by the name of
"PING PONG SARAH." While on board, I
was given a guided tour of this 80-foot
monster. I was told that she catered about
twelve guests in six individually air-
conditioned cabins with showers and flush
toilets. Much of the interior is covered
in teak. On the 2nd deck was a twenty-

seven inch TV/video setup. The ship had first class service, as well as it own bartender. The dive deck had a fresh water shower for after dives. "I thought my apartment was big."

Shawn finally showed up at the end of the tour, and asked if I was ready to start having some fun. It didn't take long for us to reach the site. We geared up and took a plunge into the water. On the way down, we caught sight of Grunts, Goatfish, and both schooling and solitary Blue Tang.

The colors from the fish shimmered from the sunlight that pierced through the water. It was such a beautiful sight, seeing the different types of fish and their reflective colors, such a relaxing place to be right now. We stayed down for only twenty minutes. Then Shawn signaled to go back up. I hesitated for a few minutes just to absorb the peacefulness of the underwater life.

As we made our way up we saw a bright flash of light that came from the surface, exactly where the yacht was.

That's right, was, because that flash was the explosion of his yacht. When we reached the surface, we searched for any survivors, but found none. Eight crew members suffered the fate of being in the right place at the wrong time. I would say that this looks like a message for Shawn.

We bobbed around in the water for a few hours until the coast guard arrived. We

were fished out of the water, and were
asked a few questions. I didn't have much
to tell them, and apparently neither did
Shawn.

Back on the shore, I asked Shawn to be
honest with me. Again, he claimed to know
nothing of what happened, and said that he
wanted to be alone. Figuring that space
was probably the best thing for him right
now, I caught a cab back to the hotel.

Later that night I called Catherine. She
said that she would be leaving tomorrow,
and wanted to spend her last night on the
island with me. I told her that a ro-
mantic night with just the two of us and
a bottle of champagne is just what the
doctor ordered.

When she arrived we sat around and
talked about each other's future. She
said that she liked her job, and would be
flying the friendly skies for a while. She
liked the freedom of moving around with no
cares. Then she said, "It's nice that my
life isn't nailed to a dead end job and a
lazy husband who had plastic surgery done
on his hand so the remote control would
always be at his fingertips. While five
or six kids ran around the house smelling
like someone needs to call the sewage
company about a leak." I laughed as she
went on.

She tried to switch the conversation on
me, but I had other things on my mind,
like sweat, lipstick, and some whipped

cream. Just joking, I don't like whipped cream.

Our glasses found their way to the table, as we found our way into each other's arms.

That night seemed to go on and on and on forever before the sun rose and the morning came. She rolled over and woke me up with a sweet morning kiss, before heading to the shower. I got up and went into the kitchen. As a farewell gift, I fixed breakfast. "I'll let you know right now, there's nothing more easy to fix than a bowl of cereal.

Just add milk and you got yourself some breakfast."

Later, we got dressed and went to the airport. The both of us were quiet on the way there, mostly some small talk here and there seemed to come out of our mouths. We soon arrived at the airport and I had no idea what to say. I took a deep breath, then opened my mouth, but nothing came out, so I remained silent while I took her luggage inside. I walked to one of the waiting benches while she checked in. After that, she walked up to me and said, "Well, looks like this is goodbye. Will you ever contact me sometimes, or should I consider this as one of those short love affairs?"

I smiled for a second and then said, "You should be a mind reader, because I was about to ask you the same thing. Yes, I will contact you." Being satisfied

with this response, she gave me a kiss,
then turned around, and walked away. I
stood there for a few seconds to reflect
on what had just happened, then I turned
around and started walking. Feeling de-
prived of a little sleep; I headed back
to the hotel to rest up before going to
Shawn's tournament.

The alarm sounded around 6:35 p.m., and
I jumped straight up out of the bed from
a deep sleep. I went to take a shower
when the telephone rang, it was Shawn.
He called to apologize for his actions
before, and said that he has a lot of
stress because of the tournament. He said
that this tournament meant so much to him.
Therefore, I told him that I understood,
and would be there in about an hour.

As my cab approached the coliseum, I got
a quick glance at Shawn being forced into
a car by two people, then driven away in
a black Mercedes Benz. I told the cab
driver to follow the car. I knew something
like this was going to happen, and I did
nothing earlier to try and prevent it.

I'll blame myself if something happens
to him.

As we were following the car, I asked
the cab driver to call in to his station,
to see if we could get some assistance
from the police. He hesitated at first,
but when I explained to him what had
taken place he said, "This is like one of
those American movies, I want to play the

part of Starski and you can be Hutch. OK.
Hutch, let's get some bad guys."
   I thought, "Man is this guy for real or
what?"
   Anyway, we drove to the marina, near an
old cannery. I waited in the car, until
they had taken Shawn aboard a fishing
boat or some kind of a big ship. I turned
to the cab driver and said, "Wait until
the police come, so you can explain the
situation to them."
   He said, "Who's going to pay for the
fare! I don't trust you Americans, every
time something happens, I'm stuck with
the bill!"
   I cut him off and said, "Look, I don't
give a damn about your stupid cab fare!
My buddy is on that boat and about to
get shot or something, and I'm out here
arguing with a stupid cab driver who
thinks he's Starski!" I pulled myself together then said, "Just stay here and wait
for the police, please. You'll get your
cab fare."
   He paused and said, "OK."
   I began making my way up to the boat;
sweat was dripping from my face. I started
thinking about being at the gun range. I
was hoping that I had enough practice,
because here is where it counts. I slowly
stepped onto the boat where I saw one of
the guards, with his back facing me. So,
without making a sound, I rushed him from
behind, punched him in the ribs, spun him
around, karate chopped him in the throat,

and swiftly kicked him in the groin! I
thought to myself, "Man, this guy's future
kids will probably be mad at me for having
knots upside their heads."

After hiding him, I made my way down
to the lower deck. As I got down to the
bottom of the ladder, I could hear the
sirens from the police cars. I looked
into the first cabin and saw Shawn and two
other guys talking. Figuring I would get
to the bottom of all this I stuck my ear
to the door and listened. They must have
been deep into this conversation, because
they didn't hear the police outside.

In the middle of the conversation one
of the guys smacked Shawn around several
times and continuously yelled, "Where's
Mr. H's money!" That's all I needed to
put two and two together, now for the
tricky part. How do I get these guys away
form Shawn without getting us both shot?
Well you know what they say: "Ask and you
shall receive!"

The officer in charge got on his
bullhorn and said, "Come out with your
hands up, we've got you surrounded!"

Being aware of this, the two men rushed
to the door. After the first one ran out
I kicked the second guy into the room,
locked the door, and held him at gunpoint.
I made him untie Shawn and told him,
"Now back the hell up!" He was stunned.
I looked him dead in the eyes and said,
"Listen, there's only two ways this can
end. The easy way or the hard way! I don't

know about you, but either way my partner and I are leaving alive!"

. He had this strange look in his eyes and said, "I don't care if you two punks get away, I'll find you guys in the end and before I kill the both of you, you're going to get beat so bad you'll wish you were dead! Because no one interferes with my business, especially you!"

At this point, I got tired of listening to the man so I   hit him over the head with the pistol. He was knocked out cold. I said to Shawn, "Come on, let's get out of here!" We stepped out of the cabin and were about to go up the ladder when, all of a sudden, Shawn pushed me down! I heard a gunshot, then several others! After the last shot there was an eerie silence.

My ears were ringing for a second, then I wondered if Shawn was probably dead. I looked up to see several policemen standing around us. Shawn got up and said that he was OK, but he had taken a hit in the shoulder. The medics came down shortly thereafter to take us to the ambulance to look us over.

I asked Shawn that when he felt better to please explain to me what had happened in his past to get us here.   He said before I leave, I would know everything.

So here I am, sitting at the airport, waiting for my flight. "I guess you readers are curious to know what he told me, yes? OK.

After Shawn had lost Sarah to cancer, back when he was in college, he started borrowing money from the wrong people. When it came time to pay, Shawn ran with about 2.5 million of the mob's money. "For 2.5 million I'd run too." Afterwards he made a few investments, which landed him on easy street. Somehow, word got out and back to Mr. H, and he wanted payback.

As for the two guys on the ship, the one that shot Shawn, was shot by the police. The one guy I pushed back into the cabin, well, that was Mr. H. He was also shot by the police when he ran out of the room waving his gun.

There it is. Now you know the story too, and when I get home so will Shelly, maybe.

CHAPTER
4

SORE LOSER

There I was, trapped in an alley, surrounded by a group of gunmen. For every one of my shots, there seemed to be ten more coming my way. I was running out of places to go, as well as bullets. "If this was a movie I wouldn't have to worry about reloading." I looked around for my escape route and found the back entrance to a gay bar. "If you're going to run from someone, then a bar named 'The Slippery Sword' is a good place to go."

I waited for them to stop before I made my move. One of the guys told them to hold their fire, then he said, "B! you have no place to run to. Give up, and save yourself the humiliation of being gunned down like a dog." Humiliation is where we all were heading. Especially since I was about to make my getaway in that bar. I told them I would be coming out and to hold their fire. I started walking out, moving slow enough to time my actions. They all looked confident that it was

over. Their guns were lowered and a grin
appeared on all their faces. This was my
cue to make a break for the door.

I ran so fast that Carl Lewis would have
wanted my autograph for being the fastest
man in the world. Bullets were flying everywhere, barely missing me by a hair. I
was so full of adrenaline that if I would
have gotten hit, I would not have known
it until later. Everything seemed to be
in slow motion as I got closer and closer
to the door. Step after step seemed to be
in sync with my heart. Thundering sounds
ringing through my ears. All I needed
right now is to slip and fall and that
would be the end of me.

Once inside, I continued to run through
the bar. I had only two things on my mind,
that was to survive this situation, and
the other was to not be seen by anyone
who might know me.

As I sprinted my way to another door,
I was handed a phone number by some guy
who said, "Call me Lewis!" Too afraid to
laugh or even try to explain, I continued
on until I reached another door, which I
entered with no caution.

I then passed through some curtains and
saw a flash of light, so I stopped. What
I saw next made me think to myself that
this has got to be a dream, because on the
other side of those curtains was a male
stripper club. Somehow I became the next
attraction on stage. I had never seen so
many women gathered together in one place.

One of the women in the front told me to
take all my clothes off, so she could put
all her hard earned money where it be-
longed. So I thought, "You have got to be
kidding me, not even my best day would I
strip for a bunch of sex hungry women."

  That's when it happened. I can't explain
it, but at that moment I was standing
there in my boxers. The ones with the
happy face on the front that said 'smile
if you like me'. Now I know I'm dreaming.
The women started clapping and making
sexual comments like "There's a case
at my house that needs to be solved,"
or "Lock me up baby, I've been a bad
girl." I wasn't about to start dancing,
so I started looking around for the one
door that's been popping up. As soon as
I spotted it, I headed straight for it.
Halfway through the door I paused for a
second, looked back and said, "We'll have
to do this again when I'm feeling a little
more sexy."

  "There's no telling what I'm in for
next." Passing through another set of
curtains, I found myself on a T.V. set.
Where an ongoing commercial was taking
place. I walked closer to get a better
view of what was going on. "Come on down
sir, you can be the next contestant to
prove to our audience that our dog food
is good enough for human consumption as it
is for dogs." I looked around to see who
was the fool that was being volunteered
for such a stupid commercial. Realizing

that I was the only one standing, I tried
to sit down, but was being cheered on by
the crowd. Feeling pressured, I decided
to do it. "Besides, what could happen in
a dog food commercial." As I'm walking
towards the stage, he goes into his spiel
about how healthy this food is. As soon
as I stand beside him he said to the audience, "Just to make this interesting
I'll give our participant here a choice
of two things. Are you ready?" He then
reaches into his pocket and pulls out a
gun, and says, "In my right hand is a
gun, and in my left hand is a spoonful
of dog food laced with acid." Thinking to
myself I realized that his voice sounded
familiar. I then remembered it was the
guy in the beginning of my dream, the one
who halted the gunfire. "You didn't think
you were going to get away from me that
easily, did you? The clock is ticking
so make your choice." While all of this
is happening, the crowd is cheering me.
The time was counting down 9, 8, 7, 6.
Thinking that this part of the dream
has lasted too long, I questioned myself
about if this was a real dream or not.
The counter started to speed up 5,4,3,2.
I looked at the audience who was counting
down with the clock. I closed my eyes and
listened to the last count 1. There was a
pause for a second, then BUZZZZZZZ! was
the sound of my alarm clock that woke me
up.

"Considering my dream, I had a feeling today was not going to be my day." I got myself dressed, had my usual breakfast, Total Raisin Brand and a donut. Then I headed out the door to try and cash in on any assignment that was going to make me rich.

I arrived at my office, or should I say the box that looks like an office. I was there no longer than thirty minutes when I got a knock at the door. It was the building's landlord reminding me that my office rent was due soon. So I reached in my desk and pulled out my checkbook, and wrote a check for the balance and said, "You can take this check now, or I can write you another for one million dollars, but neither one will be worth anything until I get some money in the bank."

Mr. Brent, which was the landlord's name, looked at me with that look that he's always given me. Then he said, "I may look like I care about your problems, but really I don't." Then he just turned and started whistling as he left.

Not one minute went by when someone knocked on the door. I said, "I'm on my way to the dessert to let the vultures peck the life out of me. If you're a bill collector, you're too late!" The door opens and in walks the most stunning long legs I've ever seen, the woman was nice too.

She said, "I obviously walked in at the right time, because I have a job for you

that might get the vultures to leave you
alone for awhile." I wondered to myself,
what kind of job could I possibly be
risking my life for. With any luck I'll
only have to walk her dog or feed her cat
while she's gone out of town. She looked
at me as if she knew I was curious and
contemplating in my head what the job
was. Then she said, "I don't have a dog
or a cat, but if you want the job all you
have to do is investigate and find out
who's been vandalizing my girls' dressing
rooms."

"Girls," I thought, as well as "how did
she know I was thinking about a dog and a
cat?"

Anyway, I asked her what she meant about
her girls. She said, "We are shooting
the Miss Calendar Girl Swimsuit issue for
Lovewit Magazines, and for the past three
days things have been coming up missing
and being destroyed. All I want you to
do is keep a low profile while you're on
the set, and try to find out who's doing
this." It sounded like your regular ven-
geance case. I figured whoever it was,
didn't want to harm anyone, or I would
also be investigating a murder. I told
her I would take the job, if the price
was right. She had no problem with money
so I was on the job.

The next day I arrived at the set to
meet those pair of legs that had hired
me. I told the cab driver to ask the gate
guard for directions. He had already been

informed of my coming, so as soon as we pulled up he told us where to go. Funny enough, I forgot her name so I asked the guard to refresh my memory. He bent down to the window, smiled and said, "Her name is Miss Lovewit. Like Lovewit Magazine." I then said, "I was just testing you. She hired me, I knew that." I told the cab driver to go before I got mad. Soon as we drove away I stuck my head out of the window and said, "Make sure you do your job, and I hope your legs get tired of standing. RENT-A-COP!"

I walked into her office with a look on my face that said I was ready for business. We sat down and talked more about the case. Afterwards she said that since I was working for her I should be at her disposal at a moment's notice, so I would need my own set of wheels. She offered me one of her cars. It was under the conditions that as long as I was working for her the car would be mine. "She knew a responsible and skilled detective when she saw one." Is what I thought while thinking of what kind of car would I be driving.

I could also feel the love when she said, "Now get out of here! and go do what I'm paying you for!" I think she likes me.

Down in the parking lot I looked around for row 2 space 1. Once there I felt that it had to be a mistake. Because in that spot was a Ferrari 360 Modena. "Life is

good." The exterior was black with gold
flake crystals, five point chrome wheels,
dual exhaust, and a luggage rack on the
back for those days that you just want
to get away. The interior was dark gray,
black leather seats, and yes, you guessed
it, dice on the rear view mirror.

At the same time that I was foaming
at the mouth, Shelly was out on her own
case. She was asked to investigate some
strange sightings in a field near Carl's
Beck landing strip. There had been some
sightings of people appearing and disap-
pearing in the field as well as strange
lights flashing during the middle of the
night. "Sounds to me like a UFO or the
government dumping toxic waste."

She decided to start off her footwork
by going out to the field to see if there
were any traces of evidence to support
the claims. Searching the woods by herself
was going to be a long and self motivated
job.

I got myself together and walked over
to ask a few of the ladies a couple of
questions about what had happened. To
my surprise the set was swarming with
two-piece bikinis, thongs and so much
loveliness. I approached a group of ladies
who had just finished oiling themselves
down for their next photo shoot. I asked
them if they knew who's rooms had been
vandalized. One of the females filled me
in on the details and directed me where
to go. Before going to the room she told

me that I was welcomed to stick around for the wet T-shirt battle between her and a few of the other girls. How could I say no to such a tempting offer. "I heard that those battles can get awfully wild, all the way to the extreme of T-shirts tearing, or things breaking, but I'll have to take a rain check this time." Besides, I have work to do right now.

The first room I entered was a mess. Everything was either broken or cut up. There was also a message on the wall in spray paint that said, "I was suppose to win! All must die!" If I had to guess, I would say that the vandal is an old contestant, but that's just a guess. Basically all the other rooms on the floor had the same thing written on them. All except for one room, that was at the end of the hall. That room remained in its original arrangement. Not a picture out of place. The thing I noticed that was strange about the place, was the sight of one red rose that had been placed on the dressing room table recently. There was still some life left in the rose.

I continued my investigation around the grounds but found no other signs of foul play. I had to find out who this person was before something worse happened. "Help me! Help me! were the sounds I heard coming through the window.

It was one of the ladies from the photo shoot. She was on the back of a runaway horse with nothing on but that two piece bikini. "There's something that you don't see every day at a photo shoot." I had to act quickly before the horse made his way off the set and into traffic. The only thing in sight was a golf cart and a unicycle. I got into the cart and headed towards the gate. I took a short cut through the parking lot to cut them off near the front entrance. The horse was heading my way, and he looked like he had no intention of stopping. He began to get closer and closer with no change in speed. It almost seemed like he was calling my bluff. Especially since I had parked the cart directly in his path. My heart started racing. The closer he got, the more I thought about how stupid this idea was. I was the only thing standing between them and the danger that lay ahead in the rush hour traffic. "Come on you stupid horse, don't make the both of us look bad because of your stubbornness." I felt it was over for me because there was no stopping him.

Then from out of nowhere, someone sounded their horn, which sent the horse into an uproar, kicking and bucking.

This caused the lady to fall off the back. Then the horse changed directions and ran towards another part of the set. I approached the lady to see if she was hurt badly. She said, "The only thing that is hurting more than my but is my pride." She had a few scrapes and scratches on her hands and legs, but besides that she seemed to be fine. I told her that she should get herself checked out anyway just to be on the safe side. From where I was standing I could see that the horse had calmed down thanks to the help of the trainer and the ground police.

Meanwhile, Shelly was heading back to the office after finding nothing in the woods. She decided that if she was going to get to the bottom of this ghost story, she would have to do a little research on the background of the area. Back at the office, she started in the records room. Her boss Mr. Maples walked in to see if she had any leads on the story. "So, how is it going? Tell me you have something good, like only you can find."

In response she said, "I can't believe you sent me on this wild goose chase for a few flashing lights. Besides there are no traces of anything going on in those woods, but just to humor you I'm going to continue on by looking through these newspaper articles."

He goes on to say, "I have full faith in you. If there's a story out there, you'll find it. Well keep me informed if something turns up 'Bull Dog'."

"It's been two hours and I've found nothing concerning those woods. Wait one second! What do we have here? It looks like the military owned part of the land before the airstrip was built. I had no idea about this, but if my hunch is right, I'll be able to find some clues now."

While Shelly was contemplating her next move, I was removing all the lipstick that Cindy, the bathing beauty had planted all over my face, for rescuing her. She said that if I needed anything while working on this case just feel free to ask her with no hesitation.

I then headed back to Miss Lovewit's office with a smile on my face. Once there I asked her if she had any idea who could be behind this. She said, "I can't see why anyone would want to ruin me or my set. The enemies I have would hit me where it hurts, financially." I asked if there were any contestants that she might have upset in the past. If so, then she should give me their names. She said, "I might have an idea, but those two haven't been seen for awhile, plus they don't have the gall to do something this heinous." She said they were contestants two years ago, who had lost and took it the hard way. As a precaution I thought it would be wise to investigate them anyway.

Halfway out the door I told her that I would be in touch.

As the evening approached, Shelly went back to the site, and this time everything wasn't so quiet. She hid behind two bushes, after noticing a strange noise that was getting closer. "Either I'm imagining things or the ground is starting to come alive." Out of nowhere there appeared an underground elevator. From it walked two skinny, long hair men. Not being able to hear them talking she moved closer. That's when she overheard one of the guys say, "It wont be long before the contestants will be part of the fire works show, and if that doesn't work we'll have to invite some of those sexy contestants down here for our own little contest of 'escape from the caved in shaft'."

After they left, she decided to take a look down below.

Before the elevator shaft door closed she managed to sneak inside. The shaft was 5-levels deep. "Just as I thought, an abandoned bunker. I guess there is no ghost. Now it's time to do a little snooping."

Back at the set, I was enjoying a little poolside manner with the ladies. Everything was nice and pleasant. "I could get use to this." The weather was a cool 70 degrees. The pool sparkled from the setting sun's glare, which looked like floating diamonds everywhere. The music was blaring and there were a few guests that were being entertained by a wet T-shirt/mud wrestling contest. "I must have died and gone to bikini paradise." By the way things were going I was not prepared for what happened next.

I spotted two strange men who were wearing repair uniforms. Since I was not informed of any weekend maintenance going on, I knew something was about to go down.

I followed them to a nearby gazebo, where I confronted them. "Excuse me gentlemen, but don't you think it's a little too late for repairs?"

The guy to my right handed me a work order and said, "We were ordered by Miss Lovewit to make immediate repairs and you know how she gets when she wants something." As I was looking at the work order I noticed that it wasn't filled out correctly. Before I could say a word, the other guy stepped behind me and smacked me over the head.

"Man, what happened? What time is it?" I thought to myself as I was recovering. I had no concept of how long I had been unconscious, but it must not have been too long.

Right next to me was a bomb that had one minute and thirty seconds left to go. Instead of evacuating everyone, and since I was close to the pool, I just carried it towards the pool with the intentions of throwing it in to absorb the blast. "Everybody get down! I have a bomb in my hand! Take cover behind something!" I continued towards the pool, and when I got close enough I threw it in with twenty seconds to spare. "Alright, it's OK to come out now. I disposed of the bomb."

Then someone said, "Get down you fool! It's still going to blow!" Without thinking I dove behind the bar. The second I hit the ground, the bomb exploded. "Everyone was OK, but there will be no poolside parties for a while."

While I was seeing to the guests for any injuries, Shelly was on her way back to the Atlanta Press Times. Earlier, when she was down in the bunker, she found old newspaper clippings from two years ago. It was about the swimsuit contest. It read that one of the contestants that had lost, and vowed to pay back everyone because of the loss. Shelly also found another clipping of an obituary. It was regarding Mary G. Wells, the contestant that had lost and vowed revenge. She had committed suicide. Her only living relatives were two brothers, who lived in Atlanta. Thinking to herself she said, "The pieces of the puzzle are starting to come together, but what did they mean about fireworks and the contestants. Roger's case had something to do with contestants. I wonder if? ...Now things are definitely coming together. I think I'll call Roger. He might have the answers I'm looking for."

I was on my way to meet Shelly at the Press. Once there, she told me about the case she had been working on, and the two guys who mentioned something about a fireworks show. I told her, the fireworks were over.

She said, "Our cases are one and the same. I think we should devise a plan to catch them in the act."

I said, "What act? We don't know where
they're going to strike next, or if they
plan to continue this. Besides I have
enough proof at the poolside to have them
locked up for attempted murder."

She then said, "I know, but everything
will tie up nicely if we catch them in the
act of their next crime; which is probably
to kidnap some of the girls. I want them
to pay for all their crimes. At least this
way, the charges will stick."

The next morning around 5 a.m. I received a call from Miss Lovewit, that
some of the girls were missing. She said
they had a shoot around 4:30 a.m., but
didn't show. Their room also showed signs
of a struggle. Fearing for their safety
she called me. After hanging up the phone
I called Shelly, and told her what
happened. I told her that it was time for
her to get another scoop for the paper.

On the way back to the woods, we called
the police and told them the story.
They said they would be there in twenty
minutes. "Now, to anyone who has ever
called the police, twenty minutes means,
they'll be there when the crime is over."

Before heading straight there; I got
an idea to give those brothers a taste
of their own medicine, with a little
fireworks show of my own. We went to a
street vendor who sold illegal fireworks.
Now it's time to have some fun.

As soon as we arrived in the woods,
we triggered the elevator to rise to

the top. I lit a few smoke bombs and a few bottle rockets that had a long fuse. We sent them down then waited for the brothers to come out.

I didn't notice before; but it seems that our friends knew we were there by the assistance of a motion camera hidden in the trees. Since we had tripped the sensors, they automatically triggered a time delay on a set of machine guns that were arranged strategically to cut down anyone in the area. I only knew this because of the time we had to run for cover. I thought to myself that they had no place to go, during all the gun fire. Sooner or later they would have to come out. Actually during the gun fire the two guys and the girls were getting away through an underground passageway. A passageway that headed straight for the airstrip.

Soon as the guns stopped firing, we went in. To our surprise no one was home. "Where did they go 'B'?"

"I don't know, but they won't get far." I found the control room that operated the cameras. I scanned the area until, "I found them! They're heading for the hanger, let's go!"

They were already in a plane when we got there. I had no idea how we were going to get them now. "Shelly, give me your lighter. I have a plan." I ran along side the plane as it slowly started to take off. I lit five smoke bombs that I

had saved in my pocket. I reached for the
latter door, and opened it enough to toss
the bombs inside. "There's no smoking on
this flight, ladies and gentlemen. So
please exit the flight at this time."

As soon as the plane stopped, and the
door opened, the ladies raced out of the
plane. I climbed in and was met with a
jab to the jaw. "Let's get it on," I said
while gagging. I grabbed him by the waist
and took him down to the floor. We rolled
around on the cabin floor. Soon the other
brother came out of the cockpit. I punched
the first one in the stomach, then with
one blow to the head, he was out for the
count. The other one gave me no problem,
so I apprehended him and dragged the both
of them off the plane.

At this time the police were heading
down the runway. What a surprise. "Looks
like the next photo shoot for these
brothers will be down at the police
station."

Well, Shelly got another great story and
I got a date with that bathing beauty,
Cindy. I think I'll take her to that new
club they just opened up downtown called
"The Slippery Sword." Why does that name
sound familiar?

CHAPTER 5

MISTAKEN IDENTITY

"Most kids like to play practical jokes on others, with no regards towards the outcome. One laugh is just as good as any other. That's what Kevin thought when he and his friend Willie decided to have a little fun with the people on the other end of the phone line. They had no idea what was in store for their future. A future that would change them forever.

"Hey! Are you going to help me, or are you just going to keep talking to yourself? My life is on the line here, and I need your help."

"Sorry Kevin, I was just giving the introduction.

Please, tell me what happened next."

Kevin took a deep breath, sat back in his seat, and collected his nerves. He was a tall and skinny kid, about six-foot, with two streaks of purple dye that run across the sides of his brown hair. He wore a spiked leather jacket, white T-shirt, and a pair of black chaps that

he had over his purple denim jeans. To
me this suggested that he was a radical,
probably misunderstood, and despised the
authority kind of kid. His skin was a bit
pale, which showed a lack of nutrition.
From all the squirming that he was doing
in his chair, I knew that this was going
to be a serious case.

He continued telling me the story. "It
was Friday evening about 2:00p.m., and I
was at Willie's house. We just wanted to
have some fun, you know?" His voice vi-
brated as he spoke. "We meant no harm, it
was boring and there was nothing to do.
So I told Willie to grab the phone book so
we could call a few people and tell them
that they could be a winner in our radio
contest if they had the correct answer to
the question. Once they gave their answer,
we would tell them they won, but hang up
the phone afterwards laughing. Man! I'm
so sorry that this happened. Mr. B, I
really hope you can help Willie! I'm so
afraid for him, PLEASE!"

"Kevin! Calm down. Everything is going
to be OK. Don't worry, we're going to get
Willie back. Now, what happened next?"

"OK, OK, after a few calls we decided to
dial one more number. I grabbed the phone
and waited for someone to answer. After
three rings, some lady picked up. While
crying, she immediately said that she was
Mrs. Wilson. I couldn't hear what she was
saying at first, because she was speaking
very low. So I said 'Speak up!', then she

spoke clearly about some location and some money. I was really freaked out by what I had just heard. I didn't know what to do, so I hung up. Willie asked me what was going on, but I just stood there trying to figure out for myself what had just happened. Then he grabbed me, and asked me to get a grip.

I looked at him for a second then revealed the strange and amazing notion that was just made. A smile appeared on his face, which surprised me, and then he started laughing and said, 'I can't believe she thought that you were the kidnapper that had her little girl. She even gave you the location of the money. How much money did she say there was?' I paused from the traumatic experience before saying, five hundred thousand dollars. 'MAN! Kevin, today is payday. Can you believe it, who would have thought that the last phone call would be worth thousands of dollars. Let's go get it! If we find it first, it's ours fair and square, right! Come on let's go!' I've never seen that much money before in my life, and probably never will if I don't take the chance now. I also thought it was wrong for that little girl to be kidnapped, but the thought of all that money made me go.

"We headed towards the downtown area, somewhere close to Joe's Bakery. Two streets down was the alley where the money was hid. We tried not to look suspicious as we walked in. I've never hung out in an alley before, but I would have to say that this place was the pits. Trash was up against both buildings. Most of it was scattered everywhere, as if there had been a trash party the night before. Also the sides of the buildings were in need of a wash down. Not to mention the repulsive smell that carried the stench of death. I could taste the vomit forcing it's way up my throat.

"Willie ran towards the dumpsters that were marked, just as the lady said. He jumped in and came up with two briefcases full of money. My eyes had never opened that wide before, when he popped the cases open to expose all the money in the world. Well, that's what it seemed like.

"As we were being mesmerized by the contents of the cases, a dark gray Cadillac was pulling into the alley. Soon out jumped three mean wearing suits, which yelled at us to stay right where we were. 'We're the police, and you're obstructing the law. Put the money back and come with us. Now!' Knowing that hell was about to break loose, we put the cases in a backpack and took off running. The whole time the police stayed on our rear. Willie came up with the idea to split up, but I said no. I knew it would be a bad idea. He then said, 'If we both get caught then it's over. One of us has to get away, if not both of us. Trust me it's the only way.' So at the next corner I continued

straight, while Willie turned left down a
street that lead to an apartment complex.
I had the backpack with me so two of the
police continued chasing me, and the other
followed Willie.

"Ahead of me I saw a construction area,
so I ducked in. As I was running around
the site, I spotted a wheelbarrow on the
2nd floor of the structure. So I ran
up the stairs, hid behind the barrow,
until the two policemen came from around
the corner and stood below me. I looked
around for an escape route, but found
none, that's when I felt that there was
no way out. I only had one way to go,
and they blocked that way. I then looked
in the barrow, and saw that it was full
of powder. I was also close to the edge,
which gave me an idea. Slowly I got up,
hoping not to arouse them. I grabbed the
handles and stood closer to the edge,
took a deep breath, and pushed it over
the side, making direct contact with the
two below. I had to move quickly at this
point, while they were coming to their
senses. As soon as I was past them, I ran
and positioned myself between two port-
a-potties. During their search for me, 'I
decided to hide the money and come back
for it later. I slid it under one of the
port-a-potties. Once the coast was clear,
I continued running until I lost them.

"Later that evening, as I was walking
towards the apartments that Willie ran
to, I thought to myself that something

went wrong. Sure enough, I was right. On the sidewalk was Willie's jacket, and on top of it was a note.

It read, 'hurray, he's safe from the police, but not from us. We want our money. We'll call you at your house later with instructions.' I put two and two together and figured out that the real kidnappers must have called Mrs. Wilson's house after we did. She probably told them that someone else called and she gave them the location of the money. I didn't know what to do after that, so I just went walking to clear my head. That's when I came across one of your fliers with the location of your office. I had nothing to lose, so I decided to come here for your help. Do you think you can help Willie, Mr. B?"

I assured him that when all of this was over, he and Willie would be safe in the comfort of their homes.

Meanwhile, after Kevin had finished telling me about his situation, the house-keeper was leaving the house from which the child had been kidnapped. She was heading to her cousin's place where Willie and the little girl were being held. When she arrived she started divulging the rest of her plan to her cousins Rico and Paco. "Rico, did everything go as planned?"

"No, Myra we ran into a small dilemma."

"Dilemma, what do you mean dilemma, where's the money?"

"We were unable to get it because of two silly little boys...They called Mrs. Wilson before we did, and got the location of the money."

"How could you let them get the money, now what are we suppose to do?"

"Don't worry, we have one of them. Paco! go get the boy out of the back room, and bring him here...Sit down boy. How did you and your friend find out about the money?"

"Shut up! Rico. I have no patience for this. Look at me little boy, you will never have another birthday if I don't get my money. Do you understand me?"

"I don't have the money, Kevin does."

"Who is Kevin?"

"He was with me, when we found the money. We put it in a backpack, then ran when the police started chasing us. I told him that we should split up, so he kept the money."

"You will call him, and tell him to bring me my money Right Now! Paco, grab the phone."

Willie was handed the phone. He then dialed the number, waited for a second, but got no response. "No one is answering the phone, but the answering machine is on."

"Give me that phone. Listen to me Kevin. I have your friend with me, and he needs your help. If you don't help, he will die. So bring my money to the corner of Joe's Bakery tomorrow. If you tell the police, your friend will die." Myra then hung the phone up, grabbed Willie by the arm and threw him back in the room.

Back at the Wilson's, the police had decided to set up a watch in her house, just in case the kidnappers called again. The rest of them went back to the precinct. "Excuse me madam, I've called your husband and he should be back Sunday around noon. We suspect that your house-keeper is in on this. Her address that you gave us didn't check out, and we don't know where she is right now.

"Thank you officer. I just can't believe Myra would be involved in something so heinous like this. She loved Mysha like a daughter. Whatever drove her to do this must have been terrible. Do you think I'll get my daughter back, officer?"

"Yes mam, you just leave everything up to the men in blue. We'll get her back. Just so I'll know, what exactly happened here?"

"Well, I was upstairs sleeping, and I thought Myra was in the study cleaning. I heard a noise that startled me, it sounded like the front door closing. So I looked out of my bedroom window, but saw no one leaving. I called out to Myra, but there was no answer. After a few minutes I wanted to go downstairs, but before I could leave my room, someone pushed the door open. All I saw was a ski mask as they came through the door. I knew it was a man, because he told me to turn around, and take my shirt off. I was too frightened to argue, so I just did as I was told. He grabbed both of my arms and tied them together behind my back with my shirt. He reached around with one hand and started caressing my breast. At this point I knew I was about to be molested, but someone else came in and told him to stop. The first guy left and the second guy told me that I could have easily been raped if he would not have been here. I was given instructions to stay where I was until they were gone, then they left. I stayed there for about five minutes, hoping that by the time I did go downstairs they would be gone. I yelled out for Myra, but still no answer. When I went to look for Mysha, she was also gone. That's when I called the police."

"Is there anything else you can remember about her that might help us?"

"Well, like I told them before, Myra is from South America. She came here looking for a job to help her family. Most of them live there, but she does have a few relatives that live here somewhere in the U.S. She once told me that she wanted to be here, because she had lost her child there. She didn't go into detail about what kind of a lost...but sometimes she would look at Mysha as if she was her child and say, 'I've found what I was looking for here.' I dismissed it by saying it was just her way of dealing with the pain, and never thought anything else

about it, since they were both Colombian.
If you would excuse me, I think I'll turn
in now. Call me if anything comes up."

"Yes mam I will, now you just go get
some rest, and please don't worry. If you
need anything just call on me, my name is
Officer Jacobs."

Mrs. Wilson went to her room.

On my way to take Kevin home, I asked
him a few more questions. "Where exactly
did you find Willie's jacket?"

"In an apartment complex not too far
from Joe's Bakery."

"Do you remember the exact section of
the complex?"

"Yes."

"Do you remember seeing anyone walking
around during that time, can you remember
their face...their race?"

"Look, I was only looking for Willie, I
didn't have time to make friends, OK!"

"I know that you're stressed out right
now, but the more you tell me the better
our chances are to find him."

"Do I have to pay you? I don't have
any money, especially since my father is
poor."

"Don't worry, this one is on me."

Back at the kidnapper's house, Myra
looked up and saw Paco heading for the
door. "Where do you think you're going?"

"I'm going out to get a breath of fresh
air. It's becoming awfully stuffy in here.
I'll be back soon."

"While you're out, stop at the bakery and get me a Danish and some coffee."

"Why do you continue to order me around? You want a Danish, go retrieve it yourself."

"You'll go get it, or I'll keep your share of the money."

Without replying Paco stormed out of the house.

Willie had his head to the door to hear everything that was going on. Myra walked to the room that Mysha was sleeping in. She sat down on the bed next to her and started to stroke her hair. "Mysha...are you sleep?" There was no response. "I promise we will never be separated again. When I was without you, all I could do was think of ways to get you back. Now that I have you, we will live the life I always wanted for us. I love you baby." Myra laid down next to Mysha and continued to rub her hair.

I arrived at Kevin's house around 8:30 p.m. We walked in only to find his father asleep on the couch with the TV still on. "How can anybody live in a house like this?" I thought to myself. The whole house was a mess. As soon as you walk in, there were piles of newspapers all over the floor and two potted plants were spilled in a corner that saturated the carpet with soil. If I didn't know better, I would have thought that the plants were growing straight out of the ground. "If you've seen one pig sty you've seen them

all." In the kitchen, dishes reached high
enough to stain the ceiling. There were a
colony of ants that lead from the patio
slide door, that was next to the kitchen,
to the counter and into the sink.
  "Mr. B if you like, you can come up
to my room, it's cleaner than here."
As we walked up the stairs, I stood
in the middle of the steps overlooking
the center of the living room. I got an
overcast of the whole area. There were
several empty bottles of gin strolled
all over the place, numerous amounts of
beer cans stacked on top of each other
like a replica of the Leaning Tower of
Pisa, and a platter of chips and dip that
was the remembrance of a past party. "I
feel sorry for Kevin." We proceeded up to
Kevin's room. Once inside, he immediately
noticed that there were several messages
on his answering machine. "Maybe one of
them is Willie!...Maybe he got away!...I
hope he got away," Kevin said as he pushed
play. The first one was a counselor from
Kevin's school; she was calling because he
had missed too many days. The second one
was from the same person. The third one
was a call from Willie's parents. Since
he was missing, they were calling everyone
they knew to locate him. By the fourth
message Kevin was losing faith. All of
a sudden, there it was the last message.
There was a lack of sound at first, then
you could hear the voice of a woman. It
was the kidnapper. As we listened to the

message, I looked at Kevin and noticed that he was being taken over by fear and sadness. You can only find a face like that on a person who has lost a loved one. At the end of the message, I knew I had to move quickly before something bad actually happens.

I decided to go to the apartments to test out a theory. If I'm right, everything will come together at the scene of the crime. I told Kevin to wait for me at the house, but he said that he wanted to help and he was determined not to back down. After a few minutes of arguing about his welfare and safety I gave in to his demands. I told him that if we were presented with any type of danger he would have to take cover and stay there until everything was clear.

Meanwhile, Willie was listening for sounds of anyone coming towards the bedroom door, while he tried to look for an escape route. The windows had a barred frame on them. Even if not, the fire escape was rusted and didn't look safe to climb down. There was only one way in and out, and that was through the door. He tried to lift the window to call for help, but this move had already been anticipated. There were nails in the bottom of the window seal. He was trapped like a rat.

As we drove to the area where Willie's jacket was found, it started to rain. Paco was crossing the street in front of us on

his way back to the house. Since I didn't
know who he was at the time, there was
nothing to be said to him. He turned and
looked at me with those eyes full of hate,
I knew at that point there was something
negative in his life. He continued to walk
on by, past Kevin, eyeing us the whole
way. I walked towards the spot to look
for some clues. I thought to myself for
a second, then said, "Kevin, correct me
if I'm wrong. The kidnappers wanted you
to meet them at Joe's Bakery, which is a
few streets down from here, and this is
the last place that Willie was assumed to
be when you found his jacket. That means
he's close by."

At that moment a cop car drove up and
two police officers sprang out and came
towards us with their weapons drawn. "You
two, hold it right there! Put your hands
up where I can see them!" As they walked
closer, one of them said, "Aren't you that
kid we were chasing earlier?"

"Yes sir."

"You have a lot of explaining to do down
at the station, kid."

The other officer asked who I was. I
told him that I was a detective working
on a case, and Kevin was my client.

Then he said, "I guess you won't mind
working on your case down at the station
also."

I then said, "I'm sure that if you let
me do my job, everything will come together in a few minutes."

Then the first officer said, "We can go peacefully or you can be dragged, either way you're coming with us." As we were getting in the car I told Kevin to let me do the talking when we get there.

Down at the station I explained the situation that Kevin had told me. I also said that the kidnappers had called him earlier, and wanted him to bring them the money tomorrow. I said that if they allowed Kevin to make the drop, then we could follow whoever was behind all of this and bust everyone red-handed. We were given the OK, but there were a few conditions that were demanded by the police chief after all of this was over. He told Kevin, "You know I could have ran you in for obstruction of justice and assault, but since you want to assist in the apprehension of the criminals I'm giving you a chance. Just to let you know, you will be required to volunteer for a few hours of community service work. Is this understood?"

"Yes, Sir."

"Also call your parents and let them know that you're safe. I'll call Willie's parents. I'll get one of my guys to call Mrs. Wilson and tell her that we know where the money is and we should have her daughter back by tomorrow evening."

The next day was Sunday around 11:30a.m., Kevin was taken to the construction site to get the money. Then they dropped him off. He was instructed to

stand around and wait for the perpetrator
to show up, and he was to do whatever he
was told.

I looked at my watch and the time read
12:16a.m.. "To be so much in a hurry,
they sure are slow with the time," I said
to myself. Everyone was situated across
the street in a deli, and they were also
covering a one-block radius. I looked
over at Kevin, who seemed to be tired of
standing around while people pasted him,
not knowing who would be the one. I re-
positioned myself in my chair because my
legs were falling asleep. That's when he
suddenly appeared from a crowd, the man
who had the hate in his eyes last night
in the rain. He was about 10 steps away
from Kevin. So I told one of the police
officers that this might be our man.

He called on the radio, "All stations be
alert, we might have a possible suspect
moving toward the target. He'll be coming
from the left wearing a gray jacket and a
pair of brown slacks. Hold your positions,
but be ready to move on my command."

The man walked closer and closer, but
all of a sudden just stopped for no
reason. He looked at Kevin, then looked
around as if to say, "I know you're out
there, somewhere." After scanning the
area for a few seconds, he continued on.
Once he got to Kevin, he said, "Where are
they?"

"Where's who?"

"I know the police are around here somewhere. Where are they?"

"There's no one here but me, sir." I'm glad we decided to put a bug on Kevin to hear what is going on.

Then Paco said, "Kid you must think I'm stupid. I recognize you from last night. Anyway, hand me the bag now start walking in front of me. If you do anything stupid, I'll shoot you."

The officer in charge feared for the boy's safety so he gave the word to move in. A few squad cars raced down the street and stopped beside Paco. He retaliated by firing a couple of shots at the cars. Then he and Kevin took off running. By the time they ran around the corner, Paco pushed Kevin out of the way, and headed for the apartments.

We caught up with Kevin, who kept a tab on the apartment that Paco ran into. He ran upstairs to the end apartment. That was in the corner of the complex. Squad cars surrounded the building, so there was no way out.

Inside the house Myra was furious. "Stupid! Paco! How could you lead them straight to us? What were you thinking? We'll never get out of this one. If I have to leave my daughter again, I'll shoot you before they catch me. You better hope we get away, or you'll be sorry. Go grab the boy. Rico! gather the guns."

Outside a crowd started to congregate. People were coming from everywhere.

I decided to slip around the back and try to get in through a window or something. There were two squad cars guarding the fire escape. I walked up to them and said that I was given permission to go up, and take a look in the window. I climbed up the escape ladder, looked in and saw Paco leaving out of the room with Willie. He closed the door, but not all the way. After that I managed to open the bared frame by loosening a latch. The window was not that easy. I asked one of the officers for a crowbar, but they refused and the officer in charge ordered that I leave everything to them. I begged them to do this my way. Since it was the only way to resolve things and to avoid a blood bath. I was given the OK and a crowbar. The officer who gave me the bar said, "I hope you're not planning on being a hero, because all the heroes I know are dead."

I told him, "I don't have to worry about that, I'll just shoot my spider web at them, but I'll keep what you said in mind, just in case."

After awhile of trying to open the window, I finally got it open. I turned around and said that if they hear any shots fired to rush in. I then climbed in the room, and walked towards the door. I put my ear to it, but could hear nothing. I had to see what was going on, so I opened the door wide enough to see everyone's position. "The situation could get sticky from this point."

The whole time I couldn't see where the little girl was. They had Willie close to the hallway sitting in a chair. Rico was standing behind him, with a gun to his side. I figured my best chance to save Willie would be to sneak up behind Rico, pull my gun on him, have Willie to run out the back window, and hope that everyone just gives up at that point. It sounded like a good plan, all the way until that fourth step that creaked from the floor being loose. From that moment on, everything moved in slow motion. Rico turned around with his gun aimed for my abdomen. My gun was leveled off to put a bullet in his head. Myra was yelling for someone to shoot me, while Paco just stood there in amazement. "No one move or Rico gets it," I said as I reached out to grab Rico's gun, but Myra told him not to give it to me. Then she continued to say shoot him. She would have done it herself, but Rico's body was shielding me. As I held my hand out, I told Willie to take it. Rico squeezed the trigger and fired a shot at me. The bullet grazed my side. At the same time he fired, I also fired a shot, hitting him in the head. That's about the time that the police came crashing in through the front door. Since Paco was standing on the left side of the door, the police immediately took him down to the floor. Myra then saw the opportunity to take a shot at me. I turned with my back to her and put Willie in front of me, all in the process of getting ready to run down the hallway. She followed behind us, but before she could shoot me, she was shot in the leg twice. I turned around and saw that she had dropped the gun, so I picked it up. It was all over from that point. Good guys 3, bad guys 0.

Later, the story was told that Myra gave Mysha up for adoption two years ago, because she was facing jail time in South America. Mysha was one year old during this time. After Myra was released, she stole the Wilson's address from the adoption agency. Posing as a house cleaner, she got a job with them. She devised a plan to make it look like Mysha had been kidnapped, and was being held for ransom. Too bad her plan didn't work. Mysha was returned to her adopted parents and Mysha's real mother, Myra, was on her way to jail, along with her cousin Paco.

Kevin and Willie were both given $50,000 for the return of Mysha. The Wilsons were told about the boys' family problems and wanted to help out. The money was placed in a trust fund.

I was sent to the hospital not only for my gunshot wound, but also to get three shots in the rear to prevent rust poisoning from a rusted nail that had stuck me when I climbed through the window. My luck strikes once again. Well, Shelly will be back from her assignment in Peru tomorrow, then I can tell her how nice my weekend was. Not to mention one of the longest weekends I've ever had.

CHAPTER 6

THINGS LEFT UNDONE

The night was rather slow in Frank's tavern. I'd say this was usual for a Wednesday night around 8:30 p.m. The place had a simple setup. There were eight booths against the wall, four on one side of the door, and four on the other side. Only two of them were filled with couples tonight. As soon as you walk in, the bar is straight ahead, and to the left of the bar is a small dance floor. Visited every night by the same drunk, he would just stumble around the dance floor . He could do the two-step to any song that was playing. The bartender, who's name just so happened to be Frank, stood behind the bar cleaning glasses in between orders of alcohol. He was a short fellow, about 5'7", and had a country accent. He wore a two-gallon hat, a plaid shirt, a pair of wrangler jeans, and yes, the snakeskin boots. This made him look out of place, since this was a jazz bar. "But you know what they say, you can take the boy out of the country, but you can't take the country out of the boy." This was obviously something that he lived by.

I walked up to the bar to be greeted the same way, as I've been, every time I come here. Like clock work he said, "Look here boys, we've got ourselves a real live Indian in the bar tonight. What can I get you, Mr. Indian man? Maybe a little fire water, perhaps?"

"No, I'll have a White Russian or a Johnny Walker Red...Neck. If that's OK with you?" Then we'd look at each other until somebody cracked a smile. Call it a ritual if you may. There was no meaning in it, we just enjoyed doing it. Our way of saying hello.

After an hour passed by, we were deep in conversation, or should I say gossip. Frank would hear all the juicy news that was on the streets and fill me in whenever I dropped by. This actually made a few of my cases easier to solve.

I call him my silent partner.

In the middle of our conversation, an attractive female walked in. I looked at her for a second then continued talking to Frank. She walked up to the bar and sat on a stool that was two away from mine. Without a word she started watching the TV that was above the right side of the bar. Since I was to her right, she would set her eyes on me for a minute or two, then go back to watching TV. After a while Frank stepped over in her direction and said, "Excuse me ma'am, would you like something to drink?"

She turned, looked at me, and said, "I'll have what the Indian is having." Her eyes were locked on mine. She stared deep enough to see my soul. The aqua-green contacts she wore complimented her face. She had straight long black hair that reached down to her waist, strong cheekbones that showed a dominate oriental side to her ethnic background. The glossy red lipstick she wore could hypnotize a crowd of men. The dress she had on screamed "expensive," which told me that she was a woman with a taste for lots of money. The kind of money that I had never seen or touched.

While Frank fixed her drink, I said, "Do you usually walk into a bar and insult the first guy you see?"

"Only if I think he's good enough to eat. Do you feel insulted?"

"No."

Frank put her glass down between us, which broke the static charge that was starting to create sparks. After taking a sip from her glass she said, "My name is Catherine Lays...and your name is?"

"Roger B."

"What does the B stand for? Better yet, let me guess...Big?"

"No it stands for..." I paused for a second, then said it wasn't important. "You can call me Roger."

"OK Roger, are you waiting for someone?"

"Maybe, but usually I come here to be alone. Are you here to meet someone?"

"Actually yes, and by the looks of things I'd say I've found him." While all of this talk was going on Frank had a look of amazement on his face. She continued on by saying, "Tell me Roger, what's your idea of fun?"

"It depends on what type of fun you're talking about."

"I tell you what, after a few more of these, I won't be talking about it, I'll be showing you. What do you think?"

"Would you like to catch a cab to your place now?"

She reached into her purse then said, "Here's a quarter to call the cab."

We paused for a second, then looked at Frank and started laughing. He then looked at the both of us with a face full of curiosity. So I said, "We actually know each other. She was the stewardess that was on my plane to Aruba. I thought it would be nice to come in here and act like we had just met each other for the first time. Sort of a way of rekindling things between us."

"Roger we don't have much time. I only have a one-day layover."

"You're right. OK I'll see you later Frank. Thanks for being a good audience. I had you going didn't I?"

Frank said, "I knew you were not that lucky anyway. I wasn't fooled not one bit." As he was talking we headed out the door, and were on our way to Catherine's hotel.

The next morning, I arose with a hangover from hell. Catherine was already up and was getting ready to leave. I rolled myself off the bed to retrieve the remote to the TV. While I was flipping through the channels there was a knock at the door. "Roger could you get that?"

"Sure, no problem." I walked to the door, and looked through the peephole. It was room service. I let him in, took the cart and told him that the only tip I had for him is, "Never mix rum and coke with beer, or the next morning the results will be an excruciating headache."

He looked at me, shook his head, and said, "Don't worry, the tip was included in the bill." As he walked out the door I heard him call me cheap.

"Roger, was that room service?"

"Yes it was."

"Did they put a card on the cart? That's for you." I grabbed the card and read it. She had written me a poem. She also mentioned how much she cared about me, since my occupation was hazardous to my health.

When Catherine finished getting ready, we both sat down to eat breakfast. While we ate we also watched the news. I told her that I had been waiting for the news, because they were suppose to do a recap of an accident that happened two days ago. She looked at me and said, "What kind of

accident was it, and why are you so interested in it?"

"I'll start from the beginning. It was
on a Tuesday morning about 9:45 a.m."

"How about the short version Roger, you
know I'm pressed for time."

"You're right, basically I was at my
insurance company to renew my office, and
life insurance policies. Suddenly the
alarm sounded as I was walking upstairs
through the fire exit route. I stepped
out on the 4th floor to see what was going
on. I could see that smoke was quickly
filling up the passageways. There were
people coming from all directions trying
to get out. I was trying to make sure that
everyone heard me so I yelled for them to
come in my direction, towards the exit
doors. 'Follow my voice,' is what I continued to yell. They flowed through the
exit like a herd of cattle in a stampede.
I could barely hear the alarm due to all
the screaming.

"I had to make sure that there was no
one left on this floor, so I ventured in.
I ripped part of my T-shirt off and put
it over my nose and mouth. I charged into
every office looking for someone that
might be trapped or passed out. I stopped
at a water fountain to wet my rag. Once I
got to the end of the hallway I could hear
a faint voice coming from the end office,
behind a file cabinet. There were flames
at the entrance of the door so I broke
the window and climbed in. When I reached

him, I noticed that his hands had been se-
verely burned. As I lifted him up, I put
the rag over his face to help him breath.
I switched the rag back and forth between
us to try and prevent as much smoke in-
halation damage as possible. We started
heading back towards the exit when I saw
some movement in a corner.

I told the gentlemen that I was going to
check it out and he should keep straight,
the exit was just a little further. I then
turned towards the movement only to find
a boy and his mother barely conscious on
the floor. I was having trouble breathing
due to all the smoke. So I got down on my
hands and knees to breath the air that
remained below the smoke. I crawled over
and checked their vital signs. At this
point I would have to move quickly if they
were to survive. If that wasn't enough
pressure, the raging fire had spread to
the entrance of the exit door. "Today is
a bad day to be playing a hero. Especially
since my insurance is not up dated."

"There was a window above them so I
broke it, releasing tremendous amounts of
smoke. When I stuck my head out I could
see a fire truck below. I yelled for
them, at first no one saw me, but then
I could see certain people in the crowd
pointing in my direction. They then raised
the ladder up to us. When it got to the
window, I handed the fireman the mother
first, and I climbed out with the child.

Once we were down everyone was rushed to the hospital."

"Oh my Goodness Roger, you could have been killed."

"I only did what I thought was the right thing to do."

"I'm just happy that you're OK. Well I have to catch my flight now. You have to promise me that the next time you feel like doing something so heroic, you make sure that there is a way out."

"I promise!"

"Take care of yourself...Bye!" I grabbed her before she headed out the door and I gave her a goodbye kiss. Then she was gone out of my life once again.

As I sat there and listened to the end of the news report, I heard the reporter say that the guy who was rescued from the fire was accused of being responsible for setting it. Curious to find out what was going on, and possibly solve a crime in the process I decided to go to the hospital, not to mention that I was hired as a back-up inspector by the insurance company to find out why the fire started to begin with.

Since I'm going to need some help, I figured I'd call Shelly. After the usual ten rings she finally picked up. "Hello, Shelly speaking."

"Why can't you pick up on the second or third ring like normal people do?"

"The number of rings shows how important the call is. Anyway what's bothering you now?"

"I need you to check out a few things for me, if you're not busy."

"Sure, but later on I want to talk to you about my new Jacuzzi and a few accessories I bought for the condo."

"That's nice. I would love to hear how you spend your money."

"Don't be an ass. What all do you want me to do?" I told her what was on my mind.

Down at the hospital, I first went to see the lady I helped in the fire whose name was Miss Kanan and her child Timmy. While talking to her I got a call from Shelly. She provided me with enough information about our pyromaniac friend. Afterwards I continued to talk to Miss Kanan, who was pleased to see me. My talk with her was short, but she insisted that I take her number and call if I ever needed anything, then I left.

Security was tight and I was having problems getting past them. Seemed like they had a guard at every door going in and out, but I told them that I was working for the insurance company to investigate the fire. I then walked up to the nurse and asked what room Darrol Ganz was in. She said that visiting hours were over and that I would have to come back later. I then told her that I was an investigator and I would only take a few minutes in questioning the suspect. I was given twenty minutes to do my business and then I would have to leave.

When I walked in he was on the bed watching TV. "How's everything going Darrol? You probably don't remember me, I'm the guy who helped save your life," I said to him.

"Yes, I remember you. I was wondering when you were going to come by. I wanted to thank you personally` for saving my life. If you had not been there I'd be six feet deep right now. If there is anything I can do for you just let me know."

"I was hoping you'd say that. There is something you could do for me. I'll be candid, but first the lady and her child are doing well although they are having a few complications. Now, the reason I came here is because I know that you started the fire. When I was removing you from your burning office, I saw the gas can on the floor. I can only speculate your reasons for doing this. So I would appreciate if you fill me in on your reasons."

"I have nothing to say to you or anyone else. What are you some kind of a cop?"

"No I'm a private investigator."

"Who are you working for, the insurance company?"

"Yes."

"Well Mr. P.I., you're wasting your time talking to me, so leave."

"Listen to me you low life money hustling son of a gun. I know a few things about you. For instance, what do you know about the Italian Mafia? Don't answer just listen. I know about your calls to Cuba. I'm figuring that you're tied up in some kind of scam like insurance fraud, money laundering, drugs, should I continue?"

"I told you I have nothing to say."

"You'll tell me what I need to know or I'm telling the police what I do know. Just so I do convince you, how about this? Somebody missed their flight that was on the same day as the fire. Now are you going to talk?"

"Look! I can't. If any word got out that I dropped the dime Mr...."

"Mr. who will have you killed? That's what you were about to say, right? Cut the crap. You know as a witness to any organized crime that's going on, you can and will be protected. Plus, if I were you I'd start talking, because whoever you're working for is probably sending someone here to kill you anyway."

During the exact moment that I was talking to Ganz, a hired hand was being contracted to take him out. The guy would be told to find anything that might link the Mafia to the fire. His phone rang. "Hello...yes this is Antonio. What can I do you for?...Another job, not a problem. I'll have it done by tomorrow...Anything else boss?...You can count on me...By the way, how's the weather?...OK you take it

easy boss, and don't eat to much Bazoli."
Antonio then hung the phone up and started
organizing the materials he would need for
the job.

Back at the hospital, I continued
drilling Ganz. "For the last time, tell
me what you know, and I guarantee that you
won't be harmed, not even a scratch."

"OK! Shut up with the lame
questioning...I'll talk." He paused for
a second. He had a look on his face that
said "time to clean the closet." At that
point, I knew skeletons were about to
start falling. He started his story by
saying, "Two years ago I was approached by
some guy who said he wanted to insure some
property, but not his property, it was his
wife's. He said things were not working
out between them and he wanted to help
her out of financial debt. So we drew up
a deed and I allowed him to sign his name
in place of his wife's. Later I found out
that in fact it wasn't his wife's at all.
The property was a yacht belonging to some
guy named Shawn something. The Mafia blew
it up and collected on the insurance."

"Wait a minute, did you say Shawn?
What's his last name?"

"I can't remember. All I know is that he
lived in Aruba."

"Shawn and I were over the side diving
when his boat blew up. That deed that
you drew up was almost our death cer-
tificate."

"After that they demanded that I help them whenever needed, or they would see to it that I would be fish bait for sharks. Or if I considered betraying them they would make me sign my house over to them, then burn the house down with me in it and collect on that insurance as well."

"Wow, talk about sadistic."

"I became a pawn to them. They involved me in all sorts of illegal activities, like money laundering, fraud, and just about everything you said before. I was in so deep that I didn't think about anyone possibly getting hurt from the fire. I only had one thing on my mind, myself."

"What's the guy's name that forced you to this point?"

"Lozano Cruz, the same guy who blew your friend's boat up. He works for Mr. Rosario, the headman in charge. After I botched the fire, he went back to Cuba. A friend informed me of this."

"I tell you what, I'll send my partner here tomorrow to get the rest of the story from you. Right now I have to make reservations for Cuba." I left the hospital and headed for my house to pack.

The next day was Saturday morning around 8:32a.m. I was at the airport waiting for my flight to leave. As I sat there I thought about how lucky I was not to have been on the yacht that day. Maybe I don't have as much bad luck as I thought. The announcer came on and said, "Flight 721 to Cuba is now boarding at gate twelve.

All passengers please be ready with your
ticket in hand as you come up to board.
Thank you." After a few seconds of waiting
in the line, I was on my way.

On the way there I kept thinking to
myself why should I go all the way to
Cuba? The only answer I could come
up with was that I had made this case
personal. Not only did I want Lozano for
being involved with the fire, but I also
wanted him for almost killing Shawn and
I.

The flight was rather short and bumpy.
So bumpy that I almost choked on a peanut.
Flying the friendly skies my butt, there
was nothing friendly about this ride. Not
to mention that one of the stewardess had
more facial hair than I. I kept thinking
it was a man in a tight mini-skirt.

The plane landed at Jose Marti
International Airport. I went straight
to customs to beat the hassle of standing
in a long line. You know the lines I'm
talking about. Where the guy in front
of you is with his nagging wife and two
spoiled kids that keep kicking each other
and complaining about how hungry they
are. I had no time for that, in and out
was my goal. By the time I was finished
it was 1 p.m. The bus was just about to
leave, so I hurried up and jumped inside.
I found a seat next to what seemed to be
the spitting image of Julia Roberts. Luck
was definitely on my side this time.

As the ride continued, for what seemed to be forever, I thought I would strike up a conversation with her. So I said, "As long as we're going to be sitting next to each other during this ride I figured it wouldn't hurt if we entertained ourselves with a little conversation. First off my name is Roger."

"How do you do Mr. Rogers?"

Obviously jokes were in season. "No, its just Roger."

"I know, that's just my ice breaker. The name's Rose Petal. Don't even think about making fun of my name," she said as she stared at me while laughing.

She was a very beautiful woman. Her long black healthy looking hair seemed to blow in the wind as if it was a pair of curtains that were draped in front of an open window. The dress she wore was a silky looking material that shimmered in the sunlight and hung down below her knees. It was held up on her shoulders by two thin straps. A thin layer of make-up, which really had no necessary need of being there, covered her face. Her pink lipstick made her lips look like liquid cotton candy that was just waiting to be licked off her face. As I was thinking about her, she was doing the same about me, by thinking, "I'm so happy he sat next to me. I wonder if he's married. No, there's no ring on his finger and I can't see a tan line. Slow down my beating heart, he's certainly a good looking man.

Those broad shoulders are big enough to ride me around all day. How is his mind? I hope he's not a loser. I hate getting stuck next to losers. He has such perfect posture, probably a mommy's boy. I don't have to guess why he's here. Anyone wearing a suit to Cuba is definitely here for business."

Our conversation continued on, "So Rose, are you here for business or pleasure?"

"I was hoping to find a little bit of both, and yourself?"

"Sadly to say business, but who knows. The future is an unforetold story. Things could change. So what do you do for a living?"

"I'm a photographer."

"Really! What exactly do you photograph?"

"Mostly scenery from around the country. Would you like for me to describe some of the things I've seen?"

"Please!"

"One of the most breathtaking to watch is a sunset in Florida at Lake Apopka. Truly a place of peace and somber. Another place of beauty would be Canada, at Banff National Park. Here you realize how small you are when the Rocky Mountains are looking down upon you. During the winter times the snow settles on every other layer of rock. So as you look up, you see white stripes alongside of the mountain. My most memorable trip was to the rain forest of Malay Archipelago in

Indonesia. There I was able to see the world's largest flower. I was so happy to capture her image to take back home with me, since this was the only place that she could be found. She blossomed anywhere from 2-1/2 to three feet across. It was like no other flower, because she was the only flower with an attitude. As a parasite, she sucked the life out of the host plant. Later before dying she gave off the aroma of dead fish. Not particularly the kind of flower you'd give to your girlfriend."

While she was still talking, we were nearing the hotel. I then said, "Well looks like we're here."

"I'm sorry. I didn't give you a chance to talk. Since I controlled most of our little talking session, would you like to join me in a couple of hours, or should we say bye to each other here?"

"I would prefer that we did...get together later. I have a few things to do first, then I'll meet you around 4 p.m."

"Sounds good to me."

The bus then stopped and we got off. Outside, we grabbed our bags and headed for the lobby. I had some calls to make so I told her that I'd see her later.

When I was finished with my calls, I checked in. Then I walked around and talked to a few locals. I wanted to arouse some suspicion, so Lozano would get word that I was looking for him. This was the easiest way for me to draw him out.

While I was doing that, back in Atlanta Shelly was on her way to the hospital. By the time she got there, it was 3:35 p.m. She spoke to the nurse at the information desk. "Excuse me, what room is Darrol Ganz in?"

"He's in room 210, but there's a guard at the door. Are you family?"

"No, I'm a reporter. I'm here to get a few details for a story I'm doing."

"Just tell the guard the same thing."

"Thank you." Once Shelly got by the guard, she walked in Ganz's room, introduced herself, then went straight to asking him questions.

At the same time that she was questioning him, I was on my way back to the hotel. I went to my room to change my clothes. Off with the slacks and into the shorts. After that I went downstairs where Rose was waiting for me. I approached her and said, "Thank you for waiting. I hope I didn't waste too much time."

"Not at all, besides the bus hasn't arrived yet. Would you like to read a newspaper while we wait?"

"No thank you. Did you notice the strange name for their newspaper 'The Granma'."

A gentleman who was also waiting for the bus overheard what I had just said. So he made a comment. "Excuse me sir, I heard what you said about the paper. That name has a lot of meaning. That was the name of the boat that brought Castro here in 1956."

"Actually I didn't know that. Thank you for the info."

"I don't mean to bother you again, but I noticed that your wife was with you and tomorrow at the Plaza of La Cathedral de San Cristobal in LaHabana Vieja there will be a sale of all the clothing stores, especially Benetton. This store was the first clothing store in Cuba."

"And again, thank you for the info. I appreciate it. Now I'd like to talk to my friend, please." I then turned my attention back to Rose. "So Rose, where exactly are we going?"

"To the eastern seaside city of Santiago de Cuba for a fun time of parasailing. You do like action and fun, don't you?"

"Of course, action is my middle name. You couldn't drag me away from today. I am the man when it comes to fun."

"Oh, boy, looks like the weatherman forgot to mention sudden heavy showers of bullshit." We both looked at each other and started to laugh as the bus finally came.

At the beach, I was given a quick lecture of the safeties of parasailing. During this time I noticed two guys looked my way while another guy pointed in my direction. Soon as they saw me looking at them they walked away. "It didn't take long for Lozano to know that I was here," I thought to myself. Since Rose had sailed

before, she said that I should go alone
to get the full enjoyment of it. I had
the strangest feeling that this might be
a bad idea.

There was a boat in the water and I was
on land connected to my parachute that
was already in the wind. So, as soon as
the boat started forward I was lifted
into the air. The faster the boat went,
the higher I was raised. I had never experienced a rush like this before. It was
like being as free as a bird without the
wings. My body felt as light as a feather,
and I had a bird's eye view of everything.
I was snug in the harness that I wore.
Little did I know that during my moments
of comfort in the air, those two guys
that were seen earlier were in position
to shoot me down. We were heading towards
land so I thought that the ride was over
until we turned around and headed back
out. For some odd reason I started to spin
out of control. I looked up and noticed
that a hole happened to suddenly appear
in my parachute. "There's no secret where
that came from. At least it can't get any
worst than this," I thought to myself.

Besides my ordeal, Shelly was about to
run into a little trouble of her own.
While Shelly was getting the information
that she needed from Ganz, he was watching
the news. To interrupt her questions he
blurted out, "Can you believe this? Those
pilots are on strike again, one boycott
after another. All they care about is

money. Can you believe it, this is yes-
terday's news."

"Can we get back to the questions now?"

"I'm hungry. Won't you go get us
some...holy crap."

"What! What did you say?"

"The guy that just walked behind the
news reporter was Michael Luciano, one of
Mr. Rosario's hired hands. If this is yes-
terday's news, he must already be here!"

"Look it's OK. There's a guard outside
the door. If anything happens, the guard
will handle it." While Shelly was giving
Ganz a comforting speech, the guard and
the nurse at the desk were already dead
and being disposed of. "Look Mr. Ganz, if
it makes you feel any better I'll take
a walk around and see if I see anything
strange. I'll be back in a few minutes."
Ten seconds later Shelly ran back into
the room and said, "Oh my goodness! We're
in big trouble!"

"What!"

"The guard and the nurse are gone. This
is not good.

Roger's bad luck is starting to rub off
on me. Luciano will probably be coming
soon, so here's what we're going to do."

While Shelly was devising a plan, I was
still in the air spinning out of control.
Needless to say this wasn't the highlight
of my situation. Another speedboat came
alongside of ours. Soon as my driver
noticed that they wanted to take over our
boat, he sped up. The faster they went,

the more I spun out of control. When they finally caught up with us one of the guys jumped into our boat. There was a struggle for a short time. During all of this the boat sped towards an overpass, that was full of heavy traffic. Then the driver was knocked unconscious and thrown into the water. I was left at the mercy of a mad man.

As I was spinning frantically like a kite in the wind, I had no idea what his plan was for me until I noticed that we were still heading for the overpass. With all the cars, it must have been rush hour due to the fast flow of traffic. I guess he either planned to slam me into the bridge or toss me into traffic.

He sped faster and faster imitating the likeness of a maniac that was in a hurry to kill the hero. If I don't think of something quick, I'm going to be the first human hood ornament or road kill. Out of the left corner of my eye I spotted a truck hauling an open top trailer. If it passes by just in time I could release myself and drop into the back. Timing was of the essence and my only problem was this guy who had no intention of my survival. If I live through this, Evil Kanivil has nothing on this dare devil jump.

The faster I got to the bridge, the faster my heart started to beat. I thought to myself, I don't have collision coverage. Closer and closer we went.

Suddenly I was spun around, and was being drug backwards through the air. Barely able to see the truck, I had no choice but to take a chance anyway. As we drew near I took a deep breath and then disconnected the emergency release hook from the cord and the chute. The front end of the truck passed under me very fast, then the edge of the trailer, then I was in. From the speed of the truck and the speed of my body I slammed into the back of the door with a tremendous force that almost jarred the doors loose. I paused for a second to make sure nothing was broken or bruised besides my pride.

Back at the hospital, Shelly ducked into the bathroom, which was adjacent to the entry door. As soon as Luciano walked in, Shelly swung the bathroom door open, but missing him, and causing herself to be in direct line of fire. "Who the hell are you?" Luciano asked her with an angry snarling voice.

"That's no concern of yours. NOW!" From out of nowhere Ganz started crowing like a rooster, which got Luciano's attention, allowing Shelly to knock the gun out of his hand. They then started to squirm around on the floor for it. Shelly got the upper hand, so Luciano reached down and pulled out another gun that was strapped to his ankle. There they stood, face to face with weapons drawn on each other.

"Look lady, this is between Darrol and I. Why don't you just put the gun down and after I finish him off, you and I can go out for some spaghetti and parmesan. What do you say?"

"As much time as you'll be getting for attempted murder, that's one date I won't be waiting for." Luciano started backing up towards the door and as soon as Shelly said stop he delivered multiple shots her way. Not having much to hide behind, she dove for the bed and started returning fire. Luciano then turned around and ran away.

"Aren't you going to go after him?" Ganz said.

"There's no need to. As long as you're alive he won't go far. Right now we need to get you to a safer place. My place will have to do."

Later on that night I called Shelly. She told me that an attempt had been made on Ganz's life. "Shelly I'm sorry that I got you involved in this mess."

"That's OK. I was due for some excitement. Besides, if you haven't noticed, the only time I come around you is when my heartbeat is a little too slow and when I'm confused in thinking that my life is not important."

"OK that's enough. If it makes you feel any better I got a heart check also. I guess Mr. Rosario doesn't like it when someone gets into his business. Were you able to find out anything else from Ganz?"

"Not too much, but I think he's hiding something."

"What gives you that idea?"

"It's just a gut feeling."

"Knowing you and your gut feelings, you're probably right. Well as soon as he spills the beans let me know. You got my number, right?"

"Yes, I'll keep in touch."

"And Shelly."

"Yes."

"Please be careful."

"Do I detect a little sensitivity in your voice? ...Talk to you later Roger."

After the call, I felt I needed to unwind. It was 8:25 p.m. when I called Rose and invited her to go out with me. She said she wasn't feeling well enough for the nightlife, especially since I was taken for the ride of my life and she was left to worry about me. So she invited me over to her room so we could talk more and get to know each other a little better. I accepted and was on my way.

Once I arrived, Rose wearing almost nothing, greeted me at the door. So I said, "Now this is what I call getting to know one another from the ins and outs. By the look of you I'd say it's all out."

"Don't just stand there, come in and make yourself comfortable."

I walked in and shut the door then said, "But about our conversation?" with the most straight face I could muster.

"OK while I undress you, you can talk about whatever you like." She stepped closer to me, and started unbuttoning my shirt. It didn't take long for me to join in. We stopped at the boxers, then she led me by my hand to the bedroom. I stood at the bedroom doorway to admire her creativity in the room. There were candles that surrounded a mattress she had laid on the floor. The curtains were drawn with only a small crack to allow a beam of moonlight to shine directly on the mattress. Besides the heat from our body, the candles also toasted things up. The candlelight consumed her eyes making them look provocative. There was an aroma in the air full of lust and passion. She looked me in my eyes and said, "Here's your chance to get to know me. I have nothing to hide, frisk me if you like." As she was talking to me she stepped back and raised her arms into the air, and wiggled her body from side to side. I approached her and put my hands on her face then moved in to get a taste of those candy coated lips. Our tongues met each other for the first time. Swirling around like two playful fish in a fish bowl. As we kissed, my hands slithered down her shoulders to her waist then up towards her breasts. I filled my hands with their girth. The firmness aroused me even more as I caressed them. My hands became their support, cradled in my possession for safekeeping. Together we slowly moved to the mattress. Before touching down on the bed, any clothing that remained in contact with our flesh was immediately ripped off. Finally we unleashed hours of pleasure, allowing our love to soak into the night.

That Sunday morning I woke up around 10 a.m. Rose was already up. She leaned over and gave me a good morning kiss. As she went to move away I grabbed her and drug her back into my arms. We snuggled for a few minutes.

While I was in the shower, Rose spoke to me about a festival. "Roger you don't mind if we go do you?"

"Not at all."

"Good because this brochure sounds like today is going to be full of entertainment. There will be theatrical plays on the street, the reading of a few poems that were written by two famous poets from 1895, Jose Maria Heredia and Jose Julian Marti. There will also be the Trinidad Folkloric Ballet moving to Afro-Cuban rhythms. There is just so much stuff here to do. Are you listening to me?"

"Yes, it all sounds good."

"I know that you came here to work, so I don't want to take all of your time, but tonight if you want we can go to the Tropicana and watch the dancers."

"The work I have to do here will be resolved soon. Don't worry, you're not interfering,"

As I was finishing in the shower, back in Atlanta Michael Luciano was on the

phone with Mr. Rosario. "Yeah boss, it's
not my fault. There was someone else there
who caught me off guard. I believe somehow
they knew I was coming. But don't worry;
I haven't failed a job yet. I got a couple
of leads on his whereabouts from Vinnie
down at the precinct. By tonight Ganz
will be taking a permanent vacation."

Back in Cuba, it was getting late in the
evening around 8:50 p.m. Rose and I were
still enjoying the street festival. As we
were walking down the street, two men approached us and told us to come with them.
They said that we were going to take a
ride. I looked at Rose and said, "I don't
remember a ride being part of tonight's
activities." She had no idea what was
going on. I then said, "How much is this
ride going to cost?"

One of the guys responded by saying,
"You know who we are and why we are here.
If you don't cooperate, it's going to cost
you your life right now. Start walking!"

Rose and I walked to a car that was
parked not too far down the street. We
were shoved into the back seat. As we
drove off I looked at Rose, and with a
soft voice I told her to be ready to run
at the next stop light. From the salt in
the air I realized that we were close to
the beach. We arrived at the next light,
I looked at her and told her to get ready.
As soon as the light turned green, the guy
on the passenger side turned around with
his gun exposed in his right hand. So I

leaped forward, yelling at Rose to make
a break for the beach. She jumped out,
while I grabbed the driver by the head,
and knocked the gun out of the other guy's
hand onto the floor. I then rammed their
heads together, opened the door, and ran
towards the beach also.

I ran towards a boat rental shed and hid
behind it. Once I was secure, I scanned
the area for Rose. She had already seen my
location, so she started running my way.
I looked at her and said, "let me get the
camera that's in your purse?"

"Ok, but what for?"

"You'll see."

She handed me the camera and said, "How
is this going to help us? Shouldn't we be
running now? Roger please, I'm scared."

"Trust me, nothing is going to happen
to us." I peeped around the side and saw
the both of them coming our way. A few
feet away they split up. When the one
that continued coming our way came around
the corner, Rose made a startling sound
which caught his attention. Before he
could fire a shot at us, I flashed him
in the eyes with the camera. Thanks to
the night, his eyes were fully exposed to
the light. Hysterical from his moment of
blindness, he started firing in all directions. Once I had a clear shot at him I
grabbed a stick and knocked him out cold.
His partner then ran towards us. Out of
sheer panic, Rose ran. "Not my idea of the
perfect decoy, but she'll do," I thought

as I waited for him to pass me. As soon
as he cleared the corner of the shed I let
him have it with the stick. I didn't knock
him out as I had planned, but he did drop
the gun. I looked at him and smiled then
said, "Now that we are equally matched,
let's see what you got. Oh, please be my
guest to try some of that slow death Mafia
crap on me." We faced each other with our
arms out, and our back bent over slightly
as if we were two wrestlers getting ready
for the Royal Rumble. We charged each
other full speed making contact like two
freight trains colliding. He was able
to get a vice lock around my waist and
squeezed fiercely. I smacked both of his
ears, impairing his sense of hearing. He
dropped me in the sand. I paused there,
gasping to catch my breath. I was then
drug into the water. The more I struggled,
the more it seemed impossible to get up.
My head was continuously dunked under.

Before I passed out, he turned me
around and said, "After I kill you, I'll
make sure to show your girlfriend a good
time and a little firework show." He then
laughed, but not for long. Rose had snuck
up behind him and knocked him out with the
butt end of his partner's gun.

She said, "He won't be seeing fireworks
tonight, but I guess stars will do. Roger
are you OK?"

"I am now," I said while coughing. "Time
for these guys to answer some questions,"
I thought to myself.

While I was preparing my questions, Shelly was about to be paid a visit. The time was 11:03 p.m. She had just turned the light off in her room an hour ago. Ganz was on the couch in the living room watching TV. The wind was blowing hard that night which caused the shutters on the windows to squeal. Ganz felt dehydrated so he went to the kitchen for a glass of water. While he was in there, Shelly heard a noise that woke her up out of a dream. She immediately reached for her gun that was tucked away in a dresser drawer next to her bed. She then stood up, turned around to face the door, and was then shot. She hit the floor, but made no movement. Mistaking her for dead, Luciano vacated the premises.

By this time I had just persuaded one of the guys to talk. He told me that Mr. Rosario wanted Ganz and me dead. Since Ganz had enough evidence to put him away for life and I was helping. He assumed that was my only reason for being here, but I was also after Lozano Cruz. He had made my personal list. I looked at the two guys and said, "I'm holding you two until the morning. Then we're going to pay Mr. Rosario a little visit. I hope the beach meets your accommodations, since this is where you'll be sleeping tonight." I used their neck ties to tie their hands together. I then sent Rose back to her hotel, so she would be out of danger.

The next morning we arrived at his mansion around 7:00 a.m. The view was tremendous from here. His house overlooked the bay. All kinds of guns and big thugs carrying them surrounded the place. I was frisked twice before being taken to a huge room where I was told to wait.

Ten minutes later Mr. Rosario came walking through the door with a smile on his face as he continued to talk on his cordless phone. "Excellent! And the girl...that's OK, she's no longer an issue. You did well. The money is now being deposited into your account as we speak. Chow!" said Mr. Rosario, continuing to look at me with a smile on his face. He walked my way and told me to stand up. He said he wanted to look straight in the eyes of the man who had bigger balls than him.

I then said, "Where's Lozano?"

"First of all little P.I. you have no authority in this house or this country. You are as helpless as a dog in a pound. If I want you dead you would be a memory right now."

"That was already tried by two of your men and I still seem to be alive."

"Yes you are, consider yourself lucky."

"It has nothing to do with luck, trust me. It's all about the skills."

"Enough of this! You dare come into my home and bother me before I've had my morning swim and talk about nonsense. You are skating on thin ice now. The information about Lozano you'll never get, but I do have something to tell you."

"Yeah, what's that?"

"From what I heard, she was a beautiful woman. It's a shame what happened to her."

"What the hell are you talking about? Look if you're not going to provide me with Lozano's location, then I'll find him myself."

"OK do that and when you find him, tell him Ganz is dead."

"What! Ganz! Oh my goodness Shelly!"

"Don't worry, she's still alive for the moment, I guess, but she'd not doing so hot right now."

"You fat..."

"Don't say it, or you might regret it. I'd hate for you to die before you got a chance to see your little sweetheart. Now if you don't mind I have to go swimming. You know the way out."

"This isn't over Rosario!"

He then stopped and turned around and said, "I hope not." Then proceeded on.

Later that day I checked out of the hotel and left a note under Rose's door telling her why I had to leave in such a hurry. As soon as I got to the airport I caught the next available flight.

On the flight back I couldn't help thinking about Shelly and all the time we spent together. I kept getting a pain in my stomach from worrying so much.

When I got to the hospital I went straight to her room. I opened the door only to be relieved at the smile she had greeted me with. So I said, "Thank goodness you're alive. What happened? No wait tell me later. I should let you rest now."

"B. It's OK, I'm fine now. The bullet missed all the vital organs, and I was lucky not to bleed to death, thanks to my neighbor."

"All the way here, I thought I had lost you."

"It's going to take more than a cheap shot to take me out. Besides if I die, then someone would get to live in my condo, and you know that's not happening." We both started laughing.

I spent the rest of the day with Shelly reminiscing on the old days, but in my mind I was thinking, "It's not over Mr. Rosario I will get your for this. Mark my words."

Until next time, keep the adventure in your heart.

Printed in the United States
19660LVS00001B/67-90